PANTRY PRANKSTER

A MAGICAL RENOVATION MYSTERY BOOK NINE

AMY BOYLES

Pantry Prankster

AMY BOYLES

JOIN MY VIP CLUB!

Join my VIP club and be the first to receive new release information, free goodies, and other special stuff.

Click HERE to join now!

When you join, you'll receive Roman Bane's Dossier, a freebie that goes with my bestselling Bless Your Witch Series.

CHAPTER 1

"You dropped the apple! Put it back on your nose," Malene instructed me.

A lot has happened in the past few months. In case you're new to me or have forgotten, I'll be happy to fill you in.

First, my name is Clementine Cooke, and I'm a terrible witch. Okay, maybe I'm not that bad, but I'm certainly not the greatest, though apparently folks tended to think I'm more than decent.

It didn't help that a while back I'd closed up a black hole that was threatening to swallow my town. Destroying it caused my family and friends to warn me that bad people would seek out my powers.

That too had happened. A man named Preston had wanted my power—actually, he'd wanted to exchange my life for his. Yep. *Life.* That's right. I was supposed to die so that he could live.

Well, I narrowly escaped a death by green slimy stuff thanks to my boyfriend, Rufus Mayes, who had coincidentally broken up with me only a few weeks before that. We had luckily gotten back together right before I needed him to save my life.

Because if we'd still been broken up at that time—well, talk about *awkward.*

Anyway, I escaped, but we were warned that eventually someone would enter our town and start turning the humans against the magicks.

Which was why I currently held an apple on my nose.

Just kidding. That had nothing to do with it.

I balanced the apple because my grandmother, Malene Fredricks, was currently painting me—in the nude.

Ha! Another joke. Got you.

I was fully clothed. She was only painting my face and the apple.

"Hold still, Clem," she instructed—er, demanded. "I've got to get this right for the show."

The show, as my grandmother referred to it, was a community artist exhibit that was showcased in Peachwood, Alabama, once a year.

This year, Malene was entering the proverbial ring, throwing her hat in, in the hopes of winning a coveted ribbon.

"Hmm, it doesn't look right."

We were set up on her front porch. I sat in a chair, and she stood behind her easel, her fingers cupping her chin in thought.

"I think the apple needs to be higher."

"Why don't I just take a bite out of it?" I suggested.

"Great idea! Put the apple in your mouth, and I'll title the piece, *Later, I'll Be Bacon*."

"Who said something about bacon?" My furry dachshund, Lady, said as she padded out from the living room. "I'm starving."

"Malene just referred to me as a pig. There is no bacon," I told her.

Malene scoffed. "I didn't refer to you as a pig."

I let the apple fall to my lap and stared at her. "I'm sorry, then what do you call that title? You just said that later I'd be bacon."

She smoothed her hand over her coiffed hair, leaving a streak of brown paint mingling with the gray. "For your information, Clem, this is art. Clearly you're not going to become a pig. It's an interpretation of gluttony, and I'm suggesting imagery of pigs at big feasts with apples in their mouths."

"I think she's really just calling you fat," Lady said in her sassy way.

I bit back a laugh as Malene fumed. "I would never say such a thing to my granddaughter. She's not fat, nor is she anywhere near that. Like I said, this was simply an artistic interpretation of imagery that most people are familiar with."

"I don't know about y'all, but I go to big old castle feasts all the time and eat pig legs," Lady said.

A laugh escaped my throat that time. "Don't forget the Renaissance fairs you attend on a biweekly basis."

"Those too." Lady snorted. "I get all dolled up in my fancy satin dress, and then I eat a turkey leg, get drunk off mead and challenge a knight to a jousting session."

I was rolling. Tears sprang from my eyes. All the while, Malene stared at the two of us. From behind her giant Jackie-O sunglasses, I knew she was burning mad, ready to strangle us both.

But seeing as how we were family, no harm could come to us.

Finally, when I literally felt the heat of Malene's gaze boring into me, I calmed my laughter. "Sorry, Malene. I'll be serious. I'll pose however you want."

"Thank you," she said stiffly. "Now, go back to the apple in your mouth." I did as she said. "This is going to be my masterpiece. Every time I've entered the contest, I've always been beaten out. But this time I know I'll have a winner."

"Who usually wins?" Lady asked, sitting on the wooden floor.

"Well"—Malene glanced down her glasses at my dog—"the winner is usually Henrietta Sticks. You should see her; every year it's the same. She'll say things like, 'My painting is so bad this year,' or 'My sketch isn't nearly what I wanted it to be.' It's all a bunch of phooey. That old lady knows she's going to win, and every time she does. But this year I have a secret weapon."

"What's that?" Lady asked.

Malene stood up a little straighter. "This year my secret weapon is… these paints."

Lady glanced over at me in confusion. "What about the paints?"

My grandmother giggled. "They're magical. It doesn't matter how bad of a job I do. When the paint dries on the canvas, the image turns into exactly what I'm looking it. I can't lose this year. Even if I paint a giant cube for Clementine's head, when the colors dry, it'll be the spitting image of her."

"Ooh, this sounds good. Let me see."

As Lady padded over, I said, "Isn't that cheating?"

"If no one knows it's cheating, it's not."

"That made no sense."

"It doesn't have to make sense to you." Malene gestured with a flourish. "As long as it makes sense to me, that's all that matters."

"Whatever you say," I mumbled.

There were no two ways about it. Malene was absolutely cheating. Using magical paint in order to win a contest was a new low, even for her.

"Did you ever stop to think that if you can't win legitimately, then maybe you don't deserve to win at all?" I asked.

Malene scoffed. "I have no idea what you're talking about. This is as legitimate as legitimate gets. I'm painting. The paint dries. It becomes what I want it to be. Now, do as I need and put that apple in your mouth."

"Yeah, be a good pig," Lady joked.

I couldn't help but think that perhaps my grandmother was taking all of this too seriously. Why did she want to win a community art contest so badly? What was the big deal in beating out Henrietta?

That was when I realized there was some backstory here that I wasn't aware of. But before I could ask, Lady turned to look at the painting and shrieked.

"Oh my gosh! Is that supposed to be a face? Is that an apple?"

Malene glared down at her. "Yes, it is a face. See? Those are the eyes. That's the nose and mouth."

"My goodness. It looks like an image from a horror movie."

Malene's face pinched up in anger. "Like I said, when it dries, it'll be different."

"I certainly hope so, because right now this is about the most horrendous thing I've ever seen."

"I don't believe you're using that word correctly," Malene informed her.

"Oh, I'm using it the way God intended it to be used, all right, because I've been catching up on all the classic horror movies while Clem's been at work, and that there looks like a picture straight out of one of Freddy's best nightmares."

I pressed my lips together, doing the best I could not to laugh. Malene, meanwhile, just kept right on painting.

"As I've already explained, it'll look better tomorrow."

"We'll see," said my dog, who didn't know when to shut up.

"Hey, y'all," Norma Ray said, climbing up the steps.

Urleen followed behind. All the talk about horror movies had distracted me so much that I hadn't noticed them pull up.

"Malene, are you getting ready for the art contest?" Urleen asked, sitting in a free chair.

"I sure am."

She lifted an eyebrow. "Got a plan to beat Henrietta this year?"

So this was definitely a thing.

"I've got one that's bulletproof."

Norma Ray panted as she sat. "Whew. Climbing all those stairs about did me in."

"There are only five of them," Malene reminded her.

"Five too many. Now. Lay it on us. How're you going to win this year?"

Malene explained the whole magical paint thing again. "By tomorrow morning, Clementine's portrait will be a true masterpiece. Henrietta will be amazed at how far I've come in only a year."

Urleen and Norma Ray exchanged a look.

Now was my chance. "So what's the deal with Henrietta? What's going on there? Why do you want to beat her so much, Malene? And please don't say this is about a man."

"It's not," Malene said.

"Might as well be for how you act about it," Urleen said snidely.

Malene dabbed red paint onto the canvas. "I don't know what you're talking about. I've never been so shallow as to not like someone over a man."

Norma Ray cackled. "That's the funniest thing I ever heard."

Malene shot her a look so searing I was surprised Norma Ray didn't burst into flames.

"Then what is it about?"

"This," Urleen explained pointedly, "is about the fact that your grandmother doesn't like to lose. At anything. Ever."

"It is not," Malene retorted.

"Oh no? What about the time you lost the pie baking competition and you spent five years attempting to place for your chess pie? You even went so far as to spy on the other contestants when they were baking."

"There was good reason for that," Malene explained.

Norma Ray's eyes glittered with intrigue. "And what was it?"

"I wanted to make sure that we were all using the same brand of things—flour, sugar, etcetera."

Norma Ray and Urleen burst into laughter. "Likely story," Urleen said. "We know how you are, Malene Fredricks. You don't like anybody to win over you. It is a problem that you have. A good Christian woman like yourself, you'd think that you'd give up these crazy shenanigans. But no—you just get worse with age."

"What do you know?" Malene dabbed brown paint on the canvas. *What* was brown? Not my clothes. "Urleen, you've never had one jealous bone in your body. Why, you wouldn't know envy if it sneaked up and bit you on the rear end."

"I beg your pardon, but I sure would. I just don't feel the need, as you do, to try to beat everyone. I have better things to do."

"Like what?"

"Like enjoy life," Urleen said defiantly.

"Same here," Norma Ray added.

I hated to admit it, but if there was ever a competition, I doubted that Norma Ray would even come close to winning. First off, she couldn't see. Secondly, she was batty as all get-out.

"Are you trying to make Clementine look seductive with that apple?" she asked. "Like, come and get me?"

See? Batty. Case in point.

"I most certainly am not." Malene set her paintbrush on the easel's ledge. "I'm trying to show off my superior painting skills."

The women laughed again.

Malene's face burned red. "You wait and see. I'll win this year. That's all for now, Clem. You're done."

I bit into the apple. "So tell us—why do you want to beat Henrietta if it's not because of a man?"

"Simple. I want to beat her because I'm a Southern Baptist and she's Presbyterian."

"Is there a rivalry there?" I asked.

Malene shrugged. "Nope. I just think my church should win."

Okay, then.

CHAPTER 2

The night of the community art show finally arrived. All week, Malene kept the painting under wraps. She wouldn't let me get one peek at it.

It was very annoying. I mean, when you have someone create your likeness, you want to see it. At least, I did.

Well, to be honest, I mainly just wanted to sneak a peek to make sure that I didn't have three noses or a head wound. Y'all, I'm not kidding. You should have seen the painting when it was still wet. It looked like Picasso had gotten drunk, thrown a glass of wine on it and then projectile vomited on top of that.

You think I'm joking, but Lady will vouch for me.

Anyway, the opening of the art show arrived. It was a cool, starry night. The show itself took place at the old town depot. It was an ancient building that still had the old train platform attached to it. This meant that part of the building was covered and part was uncovered. The art was inside, but most everyone was directed outside, thanks to a set of stairs that had been installed.

Rufus Mayes, the main man of my life, the honey to my cornbread, the squeeze of my existence, led me up the steps.

"Why all the secrecy?" he asked.

"I suppose because they don't want to open the show until after all the judging's been done. You know how people can be competitive."

He pressed a hand to my back, and I liked not only the heat that imprinted onto my flesh through my clothes but also the possessive quality of the move. He was telling all the dudes around that I was his.

I was good with that.

"What you mean to say," he replied when we reached the platform, "is how competitive Malene can be."

"You said it, not me."

He chuckled. There were lots of folks on the platform, and I spotted Malene and Willard Gandy, my grandfather, almost immediately. Malene wore a black-sequined top and velvet skirt. She looked super fancy. I felt underdressed in my brown corduroy dress.

She scurried over to us. "Clem, Rufus. I'm so glad y'all could make it. I have to tell you, Clem. Your portrait came out beautifully. You'll be so amazed at my talent."

More like I'd be amazed at the talent of her magical paints. I shot Willard a questioning look and he shrugged.

"Don't ask me. I wasn't allowed even the smallest glimpse of the painting before it came over here."

"That's because you're too critical," my grandmother said coldly.

"No, I'm not." Willard rubbed his eyes. "Malene, is it my fault that you can't take a little constructive criticism? My whole life, I've tried— very gently, mind you—to make suggestions, but every time I do so, you act as if you're being personally attacked."

She pursed her lips. "You would feel the same way, Clem, I promise you, if you let this man put your most sensitive work under his microscope."

Willard rolled his eyes. For what it was worth, I couldn't see my grandfather as a mean-spirited critic. However, I could see Malene as overly sensitive to the point where she would plug her ears with her fingers and yell, *fa-la-la-la-la* until the person offering advice stopped talking.

"But anyway," I said, "I'm sure it's beautiful."

"Oh, it is. You're going to love it." She clapped her hands, and her gaze swished around the platform, stopped, and her eyes narrowed. "Don't look now, but there's Henrietta."

Who was this famous woman? I had to know. I glanced over my shoulder. There were dozens of folks chatting and drinking little plastic airline-sized cups filled with Coke (this was a public event, which meant no alcohol). I spotted several folks I recognized and one little old lady in a golden brocade coat.

I scanned the area again. "Where's Henrietta?"

"Shh, don't say her name too loudly. She's right there."

"The nice-looking older woman in the fancy coat?"

Malene sniffed. "If you can call that fancy."

Willard elbowed Rufus. "What do you say you and I hit the drink table? Ladies, you want anything?"

"I'm fine," Malene told Willard as he pulled Rufus away. My boyfriend pumped his brows at me before disappearing into the crowd. "Oh no. Here she comes. Hide. Quick. Jump behind that palm plant."

Even if I had wanted to, there was no way one or two palm fronds were going to hide me. This wasn't a television sitcom, for goodness' sake.

So I did the only thing I could think of—smiled widely at Henrietta as she made her way over to us, brocade dress swishing.

"Great. She's spotted us for sure." Malene smoothed her hair. "Henrietta, so good to see you."

The two women air-kissed. I shot Malene an *are you kidding me* look. Poor Henrietta—she thought that Malene liked her. But then I realized this was nothing more than small-town politics at its best.

After my grandmother introduced me, Henrietta said, "Malene, did you enter this year? I thought you said a couple years ago that would be your last time."

Malene wagged a finger at Henrietta. "Got you, didn't I? This year you're getting a real run for your money."

"Am I?" Henrietta's fingers wound around a pearl necklace at her throat. An emerald pendant dangled from the rope. "Well, I can't wait to see what you've done. You always had talent. I've always thought so."

Henrietta was so nice. How could Malene be mean to her?

"I see you're wearing your mother's pearls," Malene said.

Henrietta blushed. "You remember. They're my good luck charm. I wear them every year. You might do well with a good luck charm."

Her tone was nice enough, but Malene's lips dipped. She took what

Henrietta said the wrong way. My grandmother thought Henrietta was suggesting that Malene needed a good luck charm to win the art competition. But that wasn't how I understood it.

I got the feeling Henrietta was simply one of those nice people—a person who just said things without dual meaning. She wasn't trying to be hurtful. But even when a person wasn't trying to be mean, sometimes their words simply got taken out of context. In this case, the entire suggestion went cattywampus.

Malene sniffed. "Well, I guess we'll see who needs a good luck charm. You'd better hold on to that necklace. You'd hate to lose it."

Henrietta clutched the pearls. "Yes, I would hate to lose them. This strand has been in the family for years."

At this point I felt like it was time to end this conversation before Malene went rogue on me and up and attacked Henrietta.

Hey, crazier things had been known to happen.

I extended my hand. "It was so nice meeting you, Henrietta. I do hope you do well in the art show."

"Thank you," she said with a warm smile. "It's my favorite thing this town does."

Malene bit out, "Favorite thing? It beats out the Christmas play, the apple festival, even the open house that we have in the fall?"

Henrietta suddenly looked very unsure. But I gave her a big smile, and she said, "Yes, it is my favorite thing. There are so many wonderful artists in our town. I'm always discovering someone new, every year. It was nice meeting you, Clem. Malene, good luck."

"I don't need luck," Malene spat bitterly.

She was right. My grandmother didn't need luck. She needed magical paint.

"Where's Willard?" she said. "I need to find him and let him know what that good-for-nothing woman said to me. Good luck charm! Ha! I'll show her a good luck charm."

"You know, I don't think she meant that the way you took it."

Malene poked the air. "Oh, she meant it that way, all right. She meant for me to think that I'm a no-good hack and the only way that I could win at the competition was by having some stupid charm. Well, we'll see how *charmed* she is if she lost that necklace."

"Malene," I warned. "You're not planning on doing anything unseemly, are you?"

"Never."

I highly doubted that. But whatever she had in mind, first she had to find my grandfather. Luckily he wouldn't let her do anything silly.

She darted off, and I found myself alone in a sea of talking people. Argh. I hated being at parties where I didn't know anyone. Sometimes if I tried to talk to folks, they acted like I had two heads. I'd learned long ago that in small towns, people had their inner circles and kept to them. Trying to pry your way into one was playing with fire.

Hence why most of my friends were old ladies. They had outgrown all that snobbish nonsense.

Anyway, I stood around looking for Rufus when I spied a young woman with long dark braids standing off by herself. She looked about as uncomfortable as me, which I took as an open invitation to say hello and meet a kindred spirit.

She glanced up as I made my way over, and her light brown eyes quickly darted away. Yep. She was definitely a fish out of water, same as me.

"I hardly know anyone here," I said. "And when I saw you, I figured you looked as lost as me. I'm Clementine Cooke, Clem for short."

She took my hand and smiled. "I'm Jessica Bloom."

"You new to town?"

"Yeah, just moved here a couple of months ago. Came for work."

"Did you enter?" I gestured to the doors to the exhibit. "The contest, I mean?"

"I've always done art," she said shyly. "So I thought, what the heck? Why not try it out here, see if I can maybe place."

"I don't know." I pointed to Malene, who was leading Willard by the arm. "You've got my grandmother as competition."

Jessica's expression faltered. "Is she good? Really talented?"

I leaned over and whispered conspiratorially, "Only if by good, you mean you handed a paintbrush to a badger and let him have at a canvas."

She burst into laughter. "Well, everybody's got to have an outlet."

"There you are." Rufus sidled up beside me. "I lost track of you. Here's a drink."

"Rufus, I'd like you to meet my new friend, Jessica. Jessica, this is my boyfriend, Rufus."

"Sorry," he said bashfully. "I didn't grab another drink for you."

She waved off his worry. "No biggie. I'm a strict water-only person."

That was when I noticed the guns on Jessica. By guns, I don't mean that she had a holster slung over her hips. She wore a tight-knit sweater that hugged her biceps, which were cut like Rufus's. I swear they were.

Wow. I had not been gifted with that sort of dedication at the gym. Jessica was seriously built. Perhaps she could give me a pointer or two. Or perhaps she could empower me not to eat chocolate for breakfast.

Ugh. I don't know. Giving up chocolate would be hard. If I had the last Hershey bar on earth, the only way a person could get it from me was by ripping it from my cold, dead hands.

I'm not lying.

But anyway, a man at the doors cleared his throat. "Hello, everybody. I'm glad y'all could join us."

He wore a floral shirt and Bermuda shorts. It was winter. What was wrong with him?

"For those of y'all who don't know me, my name is Mac Henry, and I'm the organizer of this here little art competition. The judging is done, so at the count of three, I'm going to let y'all in, okay?"

"Okay," the crowd repeated.

I spied Malene. She glanced at me and crossed her fingers. I shot her a smile.

Mac spoke. "Three, two, one! Let the exhibit begin!"

I followed everyone inside to see who had won first prize in the show.

CHAPTER 3

Sketches and paintings had been hung everywhere. The brick walls of the old depot were covered in bright blues and reds along with golden ochres. Charcoal sketches looked so lifelike it wouldn't have surprised me if folks jumped off the pages and joined us.

Jessica accompanied Rufus and me inside. "Where's yours?" I asked because I didn't want to rush over to Malene's painting. My stomach was knotted up something fierce, which surprised me. I guess it was because I hadn't seen my face on display before, and I wasn't sure if I was going to like it or not.

For some reason the thought of a whole bunch of strangers staring at me made me feel naked. Yes, I realized they weren't actually looking at *me*. But my portrait was close enough.

Was that how the Mona Lisa felt?

Okay, perhaps I'm getting a bit ahead of myself. Malene was no Leonardo da Vinci, and I was no rich aristocrat. In fact, if my truck was any indication of my status, I was a renovation expert who liked to drive around in a pickup that looked like it was on its last leg.

Nope, you wouldn't find an aristocrat here.

"Oh, I placed," Jessica gushed.

Rufus and I followed her to a painting that was exploding with color. It was abstract, more like a Jackson Pollock than anything realistic.

A third-place ribbon hung from the top right corner. She beamed with pride.

"Congratulations," I told her.

Now, when it came to painting, I was much more of a realist fan than I was of simply brushing paint on a canvas. However, I was also definitely not an art expert.

Y'all, you did not want me judging this competition. No how. No way.

But that wasn't going to change my reaction. "That's wonderful."

"Thank you," she replied, shyly running her fingers down the edge of the canvas. "I'm really proud of this one."

"You should be," Rufus said. "It's breathtaking. So much emotion."

I quirked a brow. It appeared that my boyfriend wasn't only a wizard, he was also the resident art critic. I had no idea.

"Come." He took me by the elbow. "Let's see how Malene did."

"I'm going to look around, too," Jessica told us.

When we were out of earshot, I leaned into him. "That was rude."

"What was?"

"Ditching her like that."

He glanced over his shoulder. "We didn't ditch her. She won a ribbon. There are other people who will meet and congratulate her. Besides, there are paintings to see—including yours."

"Oh, that's what this is about, isn't it? You just want to get your eyes on Malene's work."

"I want to know if she's captured the real you."

I barked a laugh. "The real me? The last time I saw the portrait, what she'd managed to capture looked like mud on a white background."

"Well, to hear her tell it, she's created a masterpiece."

I rolled my eyes. "To hear Malene tell *anything*, she's created a masterpiece."

Urleen and Norma Ray whizzed past. "Hey, Clem, you coming to see?" Norma Ray asked.

"Yeah, as soon as we find it," I told them.

Urleen pointed. "I see Willard's head over there."

"Shall we?" Rufus asked.

I slid my arm through his. "We shall."

A minute later we had found Malene. She beamed like a Cheshire cat, clearly quite pleased with herself and her creation.

Well, at least that meant it looked good.

She stood at a display that had been situated in the middle of the room. My stomach knotted as we approached. This was it. I would see my face any moment.

Mac Henry, the organizer, sashayed up to me. "You look familiar. Oh, that's right. I just saw your face. Spitting image, if I do say so myself," he said through one side of his mouth.

Mac had blond hair that reminded me of summers spent on the beach. I wondered how much he had paid to look like that, and if I had enough money to buy not only his hair but also his easy breezy manner.

I smiled at him. "I'm guessing you saw Malene's painting."

He placed a hand alongside his mouth. "Between you and me, it's a wonder. Best work I've ever seen her do. I think she's pleased with her award."

"Oh? She won something?"

He winked. "Sure did. Anyway, nice talking to you. Ta-ta."

Rufus raked his fingers through his hair. "Ta-ta," he repeated.

I elbowed him in the ribs. "Come on. Let's see the painting."

When we finally reached Malene, she scolded us good. "'Bout time y'all decided to show up. That's ten minutes that I'll never get back."

I scoffed. "Seriously? We were perusing artwork, and I couldn't help it that Mac spoke to me."

"Come and see." She pulled me over. "See what I did."

What the magic did, she meant. But I circled around the scaffolding set up in the center of the room to see what Malene had created.

My jaw floored. I looked—like *me*. There lay my image, looking so lifelike it was almost as if someone had pressed my face to the canvas.

I was glad that they hadn't. That might have hurt. But anyway, Malene's work was amazing.

And also heartbreaking.

She had indeed won first place in oil painting. So that must've meant that second place went to—

"Malene, great job," Henrietta said, sweeping over to us. "This is just your best work. So lifelike. Really stupendous."

"It's stupendous all right," Norma Ray quipped.

Malene stamped on her foot.

"Ouch," Norma Ray yelped.

Malene jutted in front of her and told Henrietta, "I just appreciate you taking your defeat so well. I know it isn't easy to lose."

"It's okay," Henrietta convinced her. "I've won so many ribbons, it's about time that I lost one."

"Or maybe all the rest," Malene grumbled under her breath.

I shot Malene a dark look. "Can we see your painting, Henrietta?"

"Well, of course." She led me over to it. I smiled to Rufus as I slunk away, and he raised his cup of Coke, which I took to mean that he would be waiting for me when I returned.

I followed Henrietta and the murmurings of people to the far end of the gallery. There, hanging on the wall, was a painting of Peachwood from the main drag. Every shop for a block was placed perfectly on the canvas. Folks walked to their cars, crossing the road, entering stores. People held shopping bags; mothers pushed strollers; a couple of men stood outside the pool hall cradling cues to their chests as they spoke to one another.

The sun was just slinking down the horizon, casting a golden hue on the entire picture. It was beautiful. It was glorious.

And Malene had beaten her.

I felt so ashamed. Not for me. Well, sort of for me. After all, as soon as I realized that Malene was going to cheat, I should've stopped sitting for her. I should've told my grandmother that what she was doing was wrong, and I should've gotten up and not let her paint one more brushstroke of my image.

But I didn't. In the back of my mind I never thought that Malene's work would be that beautiful, that I would look better than a smudge on a canvas.

I had been wrong. I had underestimated my grandmother.

For that, I should've gotten a spanking.

Just kidding.

But I did feel responsible. "It's gorgeous," I told Henrietta. "Truly captures the heart of our town."

She fingered the strand of pearls at her throat. "Do you think so?"

"I do. It should've wo—"

Henrietta wiggled her fingers. "Now, now. I know what you're going to say. It's good. But Malene's is better. Now, you've seen it. Be sure to go over and congratulate your grandmother."

Oh, I would congratulate her all right.

I excused myself and found Malene holding court with the same people that I had left her with, only Willard had returned.

"So you see, Norma Ray," she was explaining, "this is my life's work." Before Malene could utter another word, I pulled her aside. "Come to tell me how beautiful my painting is?"

"Hardly," I growled. My gaze darted around the room to make sure no one was listening. I folded my arms and said sternly, "You need to give that ribbon up."

She pressed her hand to her chest in shock. "What exactly are you talking about?"

"I'm talking about the fact that you didn't earn it. That's what."

"I did, too." She pointed at it. "See? It's on my painting. I did earn it, and I would appreciate it if you didn't forget that fact."

I raked my fingers down my face in frustration. "You stole it from Henrietta. Have you seen her painting? It's a masterpiece."

Malene sniffed. "I've seen it. It's okay."

The nerve of her. "It's *okay?* Are you serious? It's amazing."

"So is mine," she said through gritted teeth.

Okay, so it was obvious where this was going. I would repeatedly tell my grandmother that she needed to give up her prize, and she would tell me that wasn't going to happen. This conversation would do nothing more than go round and round in circles.

So I had to pull out the big guns. And when I said big guns, I meant the biggest of all guns. I would pull that gun out first thing just to get her to back down.

I lifted my brows slightly, straightened my spine and glared at Malene Fredricks as if she'd just ran over my cat—which I didn't have, as y'all know.

"If you don't give up your ribbon, then I will tell that surfer guy with the bad clothing—"

"Mac," she reminded me. "His name is Mac."

"Then I will tell Mac that you"—I dropped my voice to a whisper—"cheated."

She gasped. "You wouldn't dare."

"I would dare," I said smugly. "I would absolutely dare to do so." Malene looked unconvinced, so I did what I needed to in order to push her over the ledge she teetered on (or so I hoped). "I will tell them. I will tell everyone. Worse, I will show them how the paints work. If you don't give up your ribbon, they'll all know that you played unfairly and you'll never, ever have another shot in the competition. If you pull your painting, then you can re-enter next year."

Her gaze darted from me to the painting, the painting to me. "Why would I withdraw now?"

I shrugged. "Tell them you don't think your work is as good as Henrietta's. I don't know. The point is, you can't keep that ribbon. It's a lie. You're sitting on a throne of lies."

She sniffed. "I think you're going a bit too far there." My grandmother sighed and shook her head. "I wanted this. For once I wanted to win."

I wrapped my arm around her shoulder. "I know you did. For what it's worth, I think you've got a shot. One day, you can win this."

"Yeah, when Henrietta's dead."

"Maybe. But wouldn't you relish your victory more if you've attained it fair and square?"

"Not really."

"Can we at least pretend that you would?"

She ran her fingers through her coiffed hair. "I suppose I can pretend as much. As good as the victory was, even though it was short-lived, it still tasted a little sour."

"See? You need to tell the truth."

"I was referring to the Diet Coke they're serving," she said snidely.

I rolled my eyes. There were just some people that I could not win with. Malene was one of those people.

We were about to find Mac when a shriek filled the building.

"That sounded like Henrietta," Malene said.

Maybe she'd already discovered that Malene had cheated and it had made her scream. Probably not, though.

Everyone rushed over to her. We pushed our way to the front of the crowd, and Henrietta stood beside her painting, holding her neck. "My necklace," she screeched. "It's gone."

"Did it fall?" Mac asked.

She shook her head, her eyes filled with tears. "I felt something brush my neck." Henrietta pointed into the crowd. "One of y'all stole it. Someone here took my necklace!"

CHAPTER 4

*M*urmurs abounded. Rufus sidled up to me, and I leaned over. "I just saw Henrietta wearing it. Like, five minutes ago."

"Was that the five minutes before you decided to ruin my life?" Malene asked snidely.

I scoffed. "Hardly. If anyone is ruining your life, it's you."

"I beg to differ."

Rufus squeezed my shoulder. "I'll look around, see if I spot the necklace."

I rushed over to Henrietta, dragging Malene with me. There was no way that I was going to let my grandmother out of my sight. Soon as I did, she would probably grab her painting, ribbon included, and haul her rear end out of the depot faster than you could say, *Greased lightning.*

"Henrietta."

She whirled toward me, eyes frigid. "Yes?"

"I just saw you wearing it. Do you think that maybe it fell off?"

"Darling, I've donned that necklace hundreds of times. Never, not once, has the clasp so much as opened, not even a teensy bit."

"Well, I'm going to look around. Let's retrace your steps. Malene's helping, too." Malene grumbled something inaudibly under her breath. "What was that?"

She perked up. "I said, I'm happy to help."

"That's what I thought."

Everyone was searching. People were looking under paintings, under tables, any place they found that could hide a necklace.

"Where did you go after I spoke to you?" I asked Henrietta.

"Let me see." She tapped a finger to her mouth. "I started perusing all the other paintings. I said hello to that nice girl over there." She motioned to Jessica, who still stood by her artwork but was searching the floor same as everyone else. "Then I ran into Mac and spoke to him. I had walked by Malene's painting, but of course she wasn't there. Though I did talk to Willard." Her eyes narrowed. "That was when I realized it was missing."

"Maybe it fell from your neck then and somehow wound up in his pocket or something," I said, not even sure if I bought such a crazy possibility. But you never knew. Stranger things had happened.

I mean—who would have snuck up behind Henrietta and nabbed the necklace? Folks were milling about, but they were interested in the paintings, not stealing from one another.

But of course, I could've been wrong.

We marched over to Willard, who was talking to Urleen and Norma Ray. When he saw the three of us stalking over, he smiled, bushy eyebrows lifted. "Well, hello, you three. Have you found the necklace?"

"Clem thinks you've got it in your pants," Malene chirped.

Willard spit the drink he'd taken a sip of back into the plastic cup. "I beg your pardon."

"Um, well," I started, "Henrietta said she was speaking to you right before her necklace went missing. I thought maybe it fell from her neck. Could it have fallen into your blazer pocket?"

Willard checked. "Nope. It's not here."

I smiled sadly at Henrietta. "Let's keep looking."

But it was no use. Everyone at the art show searched, yet no one could find the pearls. So Henrietta wound up calling Tuney Sluggs to file a police report.

He came swaggering in twirling the belt of his bathrobe and

showing off his cowboy boots and wife beater T-shirt beneath the terry-cloth robe. "Somebody call the cops?"

"I mean, couldn't they have sent someone else? Someone who's actually good at their job?" I asked Rufus.

He placed a hand on the small of my back. "I think he's good…in a way."

I looked at Rufus as if he were insane. He pressed his lips together, biting back a laugh.

"Thought you had me, didn't you?" I said.

He shrugged. "I was so close."

"I knew you were joking."

A twinkle sparkled in his eyes. "Are you sure about that?"

No. "Yes. Anyway, let's give our statements."

Everyone gave a statement, and by the time the chief of police was finished writing everything down, it was late. So late that I was too tired to even think about making Malene give up her ribbon.

Rufus drove me home, and when we got there, we stood at the door for several lusciously long minutes because obviously we didn't want to leave each other's company. "Do you want to come inside?" I asked.

If we were just going to stand around, we could at least have gone inside where it was warmer…and cozier.

Since Rufus and I had gotten back together, we'd done a little kissing, but I was dying to wind my fingers through his silky dark locks, run my nails up and down his abs, clench his bott—

Well, you get the picture. I really, really wanted him to come in, but I really, really didn't want to look desperate about it. So I settled for something in between.

That something wound up having me leaning against my doorframe, arm up in what I hoped looked like a sexy pose but probably came closer to me looking as if I'd just gotten out of traction. One leg was out, the other was underneath me, and my boobs were practically hitting me in the face—what boobs I had, that was.

Rufus smiled before brushing his finger across my jawline. "I'd love to. But only for a little while. I've got to get up in the morning."

Oh, wow. He was taking me up on my offer. Maybe my pose had worked after all. He followed me inside, and I said, "Coffee? Wine? Beer?"

He righted a picture that sat precariously close to the edge of a table. "Wine is great. Thank you."

I went to the cabinet, where I knew that I'd just bought an entire bottle of pinot noir.

Only, it was missing.

Huh. That was strange. I'd left it right on the bottom shelf. I was certain of it. The only other bottle I had was half full of cooking sherry.

Not a good idea.

"Well, how about coffee? I'm all out of wine."

"Coffee's fine."

But not as good as wine, I almost said. I agreed with him but kept my mouth shut.

I spoke to him as I brewed two cups. "That was strange about Henrietta's necklace. Don't you think? I mean, it could've slipped down her blouse for all we know. Maybe she'll find it later when she's changing her clothes."

"Perhaps," he said, sounding uncertain.

I dropped cream into both of our cups and peered out at him. "You don't sound convinced. Do you really think someone stole it?"

"Don't know. I would've thought if anyone was going to take anything, they would've wanted that portrait of you."

I chuckled. "Don't make me blush."

"Malene did a great job on it."

I rolled my eyes. "Yeah, great for someone who cheated."

"About that…is she going to keep her ribbon?"

"Do you want sugar?" He shook his head, and I handed him a mug. "Let's go into the living room." From her spot on the floor, Lady watched us, tail thumping, as we made our way to the couch. "So, I might've talked Malene into withdrawing from the art competition. But that was before the whole necklace fiasco. Now she'll probably take the ribbon and run."

He laughed. "She's something, your grandmother."

"Do you need one? Want a surrogate grandmother? She's wonderful most of the time. Will make you cakes and cookies, and is only ornery when she sees fit."

"Which is the other ninety-nine percent of her existence," Lady added.

"That is true," I murmured.

The dog got up and stretched. "Listen, y'all. As great as it is to chat, I'm exhausted. Clem, I'll see you in the morning. Good night."

Without another word, Lady padded from the room and headed into my bedroom to get some sleep. I wiggled my brows at Rufus. "I guess we're really alone, aren't we?"

He set his coffee on the table and did the same to mine. "It appears we are. So what are we doing talking about Malene?"

I giggled. "I have no idea."

Then he kissed me. His lips seared mine. My body filled with an electrical charge as I wound my fingers through his hair. His hands pressed against my hips. I couldn't get enough of him. I couldn't breathe and I didn't want to. All I wanted was to melt with Rufus, to soak into his skin and never surface again.

He tipped me down on the couch, and I eagerly pulled him with me, not letting his lips leave mine for one second.

This was what I wanted, what I needed. I'd missed him so much, and it felt right. My body was confirming that. Every stroke of his fingers against my flesh sent ripples of energy over my skin.

Oh, I needed this so badly.

And then his shirt was off and he sat up and I nearly drooled all over myself. Every muscle was cut into his flesh. His stomach was so…flat that I was almost embarrassed about mine.

"Are you real?" I asked.

He knelt down and cupped the back of my head. "I'm very real, and I'm not going anywhere."

That was exactly what I wanted to hear, because I didn't want him going anywhere, either.

We kissed again, and the room surged with energy. I almost heard the electricity crackling, and I could definitely feel my hair beginning to rise. It wouldn't be pretty if my hair stood on top of my head. Perhaps I should cool things down.

On second thought…

"Do you want to go to the bedroom?" I asked.

"Yes," he said hoarsely.

We were just rising from the couch when someone banged on my front door. I jumped.

"Who in the…?"

"I'll get it," Rufus said. With a snap of his fingers, his shirt was back on (dang it) and he smoothed his hair. He crossed to the door and opened it.

There stood Malene. She barely noticed him before spotting me and marching in. "What did you do with it?"

Hello to you, too. "With what?"

"With my ribbon?"

"What are you talking about?"

She huffed, fists clenched. "I'm talking about the fact that when I left the art show, I had my ribbon in my pocket. But now it's gone. So." She jabbed her finger at me. "What did you do?"

Had my grandmother lost her mind? I lifted my hands in surrender. "I didn't do anything. I don't know a thing about your ribbon. We've been here. Haven't we, Rufus?"

"We have," he admitted.

Malene's gaze zipped from me to Rufus, from Rufus to me. "Oh. Doing a little hanky-panky, are you?"

Oh, dear goodness. Did my grandmother really just accuse me of rolling in the hay with Rufus? And how gross was that? I bit back down the bile that was trying to surge up my throat.

"We were just having coffee. See?" I pointed to the mugs. "*Coffee.*"

"Then why's your hair sticking up in back?" She narrowed her eyes as heat crawled up my neck. "Never mind. I don't care how much sex you have."

I wanted to die.

"Just make sure you use protection."

I *really* wanted to die.

This was like going to a senior center to give the old folks a magic show, and they wound up pulling out their wallets and showing you which condoms worked the best. Dear Lord. Save me now.

"Malene," Rufus said. How could he even speak after what she'd just said? "We don't know anything about your ribbon. I can promise you that Clem hasn't worked any magic since we left the art show."

"Do you think that maybe you happened to leave it somewhere? Perhaps it fell out of your pocket?" I asked.

"No. It was secure." She pursed her lips and gave my living room a good once-over. "I guess that I'll just keep looking."

"Sounds good."

Her gaze dragged from me to Rufus. "I'll leave the both of y'all." She started to exit, and relief flooded me. Unfortunately it was short-lived. "And Clem?"

What now? "Yes?" I said in my chipperest voice.

"Don't forget—we're dishing up the Thursday lunch at the Baptist church this week. I'll expect you there at ten."

I'd nearly forgotten. The Baptists fed those who needed it—elderly, disabled, poor—you name it, the church had a meal for them.

"I'll be there," I promised.

"See that you are. And in the meantime, use protection."

With that she left and I wanted to dive under the couch, never to be seen again. When she was gone, Rufus came over, took me by the shoulders and kissed me with a tenderness that only his lips could manage.

"I should probably be leaving."

I understood. My grandmother had pretty much been the buzzkill to end all buzzkills. Even I wasn't in the mood anymore. "Okay."

"I'll call you tomorrow," he said before kissing my forehead.

"I can't wait." I walked him to the door and watched as he made his way down the porch steps. "Be careful."

He waved, and right before he got into his SUV, Malene shouted from her porch, "Don't forget the protection!"

I slammed the door.

CHAPTER 5

The next morning I decided to make my breakfast for once. After the previous night, when Malene had shared intimate details about my love life with the neighbors, I really didn't want to see her in person to ask for a slice of pie. Plus, I was all out of Entenmann's chocolate glazed donuts. So oatmeal it was.

If I could find it.

Last Christmas I had made an apple crisp for a dessert at our family get-together, and since I wasn't a huge oatmeal eater, I had only used a couple tablespoons of the oats, leaving the rest.

That should have meant that somewhere in the recesses of my cabinet there was a carton of the stuff.

If I could just find it, that was.

"What're you looking for?" Lady asked, padding up to me.

"Something that only exists in the seventh circle of Hades, apparently."

"Oh, you lost something in your cabinet again?"

"Yep." It was so dark back there. I couldn't see anything. I pulled my phone from my back pocket and shone the light inside. "There. That's better."

"I got news for you—if you need to use a flashlight to find your food, I'd say we're in trouble."

I shot her a dark look and turned to the cabinet. In the very rear I spotted the faint outline of a quaker hat. "There it is." I pulled the cylinder from the back and dragged it over cans of beans and diced tomatoes. "There," I told Lady triumphantly. "I found it."

"I wouldn't celebrate yet."

"Why not?"

Her gaze darted to the bottom of the container. "Look."

A trail of oats cascaded from the bottom of the Quaker's picture on the cover, landing on the floor in a pile.

"Oh!" I cupped the hole on the bottom and darted to the counter to put the container down. "What a mess." I located my broom, swept up the debris and then cleaned up the trail of oats that dusted my canned goods. When I'd finished, I turned to Lady. "Think we've got a mouse?"

"Let me see." She lifted her nose and sniffed. "I don't smell no mouse. But that don't mean nothing. That mouse could be wearing dog scent for all I know."

It took everything I had not to laugh. "A mouse wearing dog scent?"

"I've heard of stranger things—like a hole that gives you what you ask for."

Touché. Indeed, the black hole that had appeared in Norma Ray's barn had done just that, and it had taken every bit of power I had to plug the hole. But that didn't matter because clearly we had a mouse. "Let me get a trap."

"Where're you going to set it?"

"In the cabinet. Not sure how the little sucker got in there, but I'll get him."

I found a trap in my kitchen's junk drawer. If you don't know what that is, then you might not live in the South. Every Southern kitchen that I've ever known has one drawer where all the odds and ends go—screwdrivers, batteries, small lightbulbs, tape, etc. You name it, the junk drawer is the place for it.

After I'd baited and set the trap, I turned to Lady. "How about we go to Bender's for breakfast?"

She licked her chops. "Sounds perfect to me."

We reached the coffee shop a few minutes later. Julie Bender, the owner and proprietor, was finishing ringing up her boyfriend and local artist, Thomas. Some of his paintings hung on the walls. They were gorgeous—full of dark-skinned people dancing under the moon or laughing with one another. Thomas was a pro, definitely way above the level of amateur that the local art competition had housed.

"Clem," he greeted me after he finished paying Julie. "Good to see you. Did you like the way the art contest turned out?" he added with a wink.

"Oh, were you one of the judges?"

"He sure was," Julie added from behind him.

"You didn't tell him to go easy on Malene's painting, did you, Julie?"

Thomas smiled. "Even if she did, I wouldn't have. When I'm judging, that's what I do. I don't pull any punches." He leaned forward and said conspiratorially, "Unless of course it's a community art show and everyone there is only an amateur. That, I take very seriously, because I remember what it was like before I started getting commissions."

"Hard?" I asked.

"Just a lot of worrying and angst." He took the coffee that Julie settled on the counter and sipped it. "Being an artist is a strange thing. You may believe that you're talented, know that you've got something to say. But until someone validates you, tells you that you've got skills, you don't believe it. At least I didn't. It's not a vocation that I would put on anyone. You're alone a lot, so it's very solitary. Plus, like I said, you're waiting around for someone to tell you that you're good, to believe in you."

"Hmm, sounds like it's easy to get your hopes crushed."

He snapped his fingers. "That's exactly right. It's easy to think you don't have a lick of talent. That's why I always offer to judge any amateur show, and when I'm there, I try to see what the artist wanted me to see instead of me seeing what I want to. It makes a difference."

"Not to brag," Julie said, "but our artist here has a new piece on the wall."

"Oh? Let me see."

"Julie, you shouldn't," Thomas scolded lightly.

"Why shouldn't I?" She placed her fists on her hips. "It's beautiful. I want the whole town to know it."

Thomas led Lady and me over to the wall. "This is it. What do you think?"

What did I think? It was a city under the umbrella of night. The moon glowed in the upper right corner. It had been painted with thick oils. On a street corner stood a woman, bent over, crying. Approaching her was a man, handkerchief out, ready to dry her tears. She was peering up at him as the man headed toward her.

The moment was pregnant with possibility. It was a moment of choice. I didn't know if the two characters on the canvas knew one another, but it didn't matter. Would she take the handkerchief, or would she reject it?

I loved the tension created in the image. It reminded me of life—you just never knew who was going to step in and dry your tears for you.

"It's wonderful," I said.

"One of my best," Thomas said proudly. "I asked Julie if I could hang it in here. I've already got a potential buyer for it. But I wanted it to live and breathe in a place of life before I sold it and it went on display in someone's house."

"I'm thankful that you shared this with us. And that you were kind enough to judge the competition."

Speaking of, I was tempted to confess to Thomas what Malene had done. He was a true artist, someone who lived and breathed his profession. Malene had spat on that profession when she cheated. It wasn't fair to the others that she'd rigged the system. It wasn't fair to Thomas, either.

But if I told him now, he'd contact Mac, who would, of course, take Malene's ribbon (if she'd found it, that was). My actions would take her by surprise. I would be butting in and messing with her life instead of letting Malene do the messing up. She was the one who had acted wrongly. It was up to her to admit that and take her punishment.

"Thank you for being such a wonderful person in this community," I told Thomas.

He shrugged as if it was no big deal. "I like Peachwood. I'm happy to help out the folks here any way that I can. But don't let me keep you chatting." He pointed to my empty hands. "I'm pretty sure you came here for a coffee, not to be sucked into a conversation about art."

"Indeed, I did."

I said goodbye and ordered a mocha and a chocolate muffin from Julie. Yes, I was putting the chocolate on thick this morning. I paid her and exited the cafe.

A familiar face greeted me on the way out. "Jessica?"

The newcomer to town looked up from the phone in her hand and smiled. "Hi. It's Clem, right?"

"That's right. How're you doing?"

"Doing good, I suppose, considering what happened last night."

"Oh, I know. Henrietta was pretty upset. But hopefully she finds the necklace. I can't imagine anyone at the art show stole it. It's just a bunch of folks from town looking at art. We're not thieves." Remembering that Jessica had just moved here, I added, "I don't want you to get the wrong impression of us. We're decent people."

"Oh, I know that. I'm sure Henrietta just lost the pearls."

Remembering that Thomas was inside, I said, "And the person who judged the entries was just ahead of me in line. He's a full-time artist and has some of his paintings on the wall."

Her eyes widened. "Really?"

"That's right. If you hurry, you might get a chance to talk to him."

"And thank him." Jessica started to move past me and stopped. She gave me a shy smile. "Thank you. See you around."

"See you around."

She headed into Bender's, and I walked Lady down the street. The muffin hung heavy in the paper bag that I carried. I couldn't wait to sink my teeth into it.

"Where're we going?" Lady asked.

Before I had a chance to answer, loud voices caught my attention. A line of kids on bicycles jetted past me. They were pumping the pedals hard, racing away as fast as possible.

"Come on," the lead boy shouted.

"Let's hurry," called another.

"I'm hurrying," yelled the boy in the rear. He was a bit portly and couldn't keep up quite as good as the others, but he was still pedaling hard. "I'm doing the best I can!"

Memories of days spent as a kid riding my bike flashed in my mind. Those were the best of days—no responsibilities, just fun with friends.

I smiled at the kids, but they were past me, headed down the street. The boy bringing up the rear had a canvas bag slung over his shoulder. The flap to keep all the contents inside had two fasteners, but one of them was unlatched. From the cavernous depths, where no doubt the kids housed their phones or walkie-talkies, I swore that a light shone. It was pink and I could have sworn it was in the shape of—

I stopped myself. No way did the kids have what I thought they did. They were just kids. I was seeing things.

"What is it?" Lady asked.

Jolted back into the now, I shook my head. "It's nothing."

But was it something? It wasn't, I decided. They were just kids. They couldn't know anything about magic.

As I headed to my car, I spotted Malene's Miata burning rubber as it zipped down the street. She came to a screeching halt in front of the library, got out (being sure to smooth her hair) and strode inside.

"I'll tell you where we're going now," I said.

"Where's that?"

I nodded toward the building that Malene had just disappeared inside. "We're going to interrupt a quilting bee."

CHAPTER 6

"Oh? Decided to join the quilting bee?" Norma Ray asked hopefully when I entered the small room that she, Urleen and Malene used in the front of the library as their quilting room.

"Actually, no. I came to talk to Malene."

Malene, who was pretending to stitch a patch of fabric inside a quilting square, did not look up when she said, "What a surprise. Y'all, my granddaughter has come to make sure that I'm doing what it is that I need to do."

I rolled my eyes. "I spoke with Thomas this morning."

She looked up, blinking like a deer unsure if it was staring at headlights or the exploding end of a rifle. "I still haven't found my ribbon, if it's any consolation, but never mind that. Who is this Thomas?"

My stomach growled as I was about to answer. Starving, I pulled out my muffin and bit into it. Lady, who was either impatient or just dying to spill the beans, spoke for me.

"Thomas is the man who judged your art entry, Malene. He's a real artist. He don't use magical paint or nothing."

Malene did not look impressed. "Did he say as much?"

"No, but you could tell," my dog said, sitting on her haunches. "His work is so good that he don't need magical paint."

"Well, good for him."

I finally came up for a breath. "Are you going to tell Mac what you've done?"

"She will," Urleen said, her voice dripping with sarcasm, "all in her own time, which will be in about a hundred years."

"But she'll be dead by then," Norma Ray interjected.

Urleen didn't look up from her sewing machine as she pushed a line of fabric through. "That's the point. Malene's never going to confess."

"Well, I think the truth is always the best policy," Norma said, not realizing that as she talked, Malene's face was turning more and more red. "When I first saw that painting of Clem, I thought there was no way on God's green earth that it was going to turn out pretty. Let's face it, Lady could've done a better job painting. But when I saw it last night, I was stunned. But I was also sad, because what you did, Malene, that wasn't right."

Malene sniffed. "What about what someone did to Henrietta? Stealing is worse than cheating."

Was it? Like, really? Weren't they both on about the same level? The way I saw it, cheating *was* stealing. When a person cheated, they robbed someone else of what was due to them—their achievement. Malene had robbed Henrietta of first place. She also robbed someone else of third place, someone who would've ribboned if they hadn't been relegated to the fourth slot thanks to Malene.

"So are you going to say something?" I asked. "Or will I have to?"

She dropped the quilting square in her lap. "Do you really think this is what Mac needs right now?"

"Mac?" What did he have to do with this? "I don't see how bringing him up is important. He's just the coordinator."

"That's not true. The depot is also owned by him. He's already got a potential theft on his hands. Do you want to make it worse for him and add cheating to the list? If you tell him that, there might not ever be another community art show ever again."

"Ooh, Malene's right," Norma Ray added. "The entire event will be tainted with the blood of theft and cheating."

It took everything I had not to roll my eyes. "I hardly thing we can akin those two with bloodshed."

"I don't know," Urleen said in surly tone. "It seems they might not be too far off."

"The ladies are right," my grandmother announced. "There's too much riding on this for me to just come out and admit that I may or may not have bent the rules a little to win."

I scoffed. "May or may not have bent the rules? You're joking, right?"

"Not at all. Nowhere in the art show rules does it say that a person can't use magical paint."

"She's got you there," Lady so politely pointed out. "If it don't say it, it don't say it."

Well, they had me, didn't they? But I did understand Malene's point. There wasn't a reason to bring any more scandal to the art show. People were probably already talking about how Henrietta's necklace had been stolen. If they started thinking that the competition was full of cheaters, then no one would want to enter and the town would shut it down. I hated to think that something that brought the community together would be stopped until further notice.

Perhaps they had a point. Maybe it was better if we didn't say anything, if we simply kept our collective mouths shut.

But the part of me that clamored for justice wouldn't stop screaming in my ear. Perhaps some justice was better than none. Maybe it was best if Henrietta's necklace was found first. If it turned out that the necklace's disappearance wasn't at all connected with the art show, perhaps I could make a case to Malene to confess.

Or perhaps not, I thought as she stared at me. It didn't look like Malene would go down easily for this one. She'd worked hard at cheating and wanted to keep that ribbon more than anything.

"What if…you promise never to enter the art show again?" I asked.

Norma Ray stopped sewing. "Ooh, you're playing with fire there, girlie."

"What? How?"

"Because Malene is a fire, and when a person plays with flames, they get burned."

Urleen glanced up from the sewing machine to add, "Unless that fire is coming from a candle."

Malene scoffed. "I will have the both of you know that I am a raging funeral pyre."

I had to bite my bottom lip to keep from laughing. The idea that my barely five-foot grandmother was somehow a firestorm made me want to giggle.

"You look more like an oil lamp," Norma Ray argued. "One that could easily be knocked over. Then it would consume an entire cabin."

"Oh, I sort of like that one," Malene said sheepishly.

"Me too," Urleen chirped. "It's very fitting. You're too short to be a wildfire. But an oil lamp, I can see. Lots of potential there."

I wanted to stab myself in the eye.

Lady spoke to me. "Are they always this unfocused?"

"Sometimes, but not always. It's frustrating, isn't it?"

"You're telling me. First we're talking about wildfires, and now we're at candles and stuff. I can't keep up."

"Join the club." I clapped my hands to get the ladies' attention as they were knee-deep in what kind of oil Malene might have in her lamp. They stopped talking and fixed me with gazes that were shocked that I'd dared to interrupt them. I ignored the looks. "Y'all, can we please be serious?"

Malene blinked. "We were being serious. Deciding exactly what sort of fire I am is very serious business."

"Okay, well, let's move back to my point. What if you promised never to enter the art show again? Would you do that?"

She folded her arms. "What do I get out of it?"

"Well, for one, I would promise never to tell about this competition, that you cheated. *If* you swear that you'll never enter another show again."

"I don't know if I can do that."

"Why not?"

"It seems I like winning."

I groaned. Seriously? Malene had won her ribbon unfairly, and now she was addicted to the feeling? *Someone please put me out of my misery.*

"You can't be serious," I said. "You used magical paint to gain that ribbon, cheating Henrietta and goodness knows who else out of a victory. You can't keep doing that."

"For all I know, Henrietta cheated, too," Malene replied, hitting each word with gusto.

"What are you talking about?"

"She's Presbyterian." Malene said it confidentially, as if she was revealing some huge secret. "That's all I'm going to say."

I stood, dumbstruck. "And what exactly does that mean?"

"It means she may have cheated," Norma Ray interpreted for me.

"I get that. But I don't understand what her religious affiliation has to do with anything."

The three women exchanged a look. It was Urleen who finally spoke. "You wouldn't understand because you haven't lived here as long as we have. But let me assure you that the Presbyterians and the Baptists have been at each other's throats for as long as time has existed."

Somehow I doubted that.

"They always try to one-up us," Norma Ray explained. "If we have a bake-off, they try to make theirs better. If we have a float in a parade, they try to outdo it. There always has been competition."

"So you see," Malene added, "any occasion for one of their kind to win, they'll take it. The art show is no exception. Like I said, I wouldn't have been surprised if a bunch of those ladies got together and helped Henrietta paint her canvas. They've probably been doing it for years."

I rolled my eyes. "Aren't y'all being a little ridiculous?"

"No," they said in unison.

"You just haven't seen it," Urleen added.

And that came from the most thoughtful person of the bunch. If Urleen believed that the Presbyterians were up to some funny business, maybe they were.

No. Wait. I couldn't go there. I couldn't get sucked down the crazy train that those three were on. I needed to stay on my even-keeled plane of existence.

"You just watch," Malene said. "They're having a feed-the-hungry pantry lunch the same day we are. They'll probably do what they can to make theirs look better than ours."

"I doubt it," I whispered.

Lady stepped on my foot. She glanced up at me, her eyes full of warning. Even she thought going against their crazy theories was dangerous territory.

Maybe she was right.

"Okay, fine. Any and all conspiracy theories in Peachwood feature the Presbyterians. They probably had a hand in killing JFK, too."

"No, that was the mafia," Malene said matter-of-factly.

"Of course it was." I clapped my hands. "It's been fun chatting. Malene, think about what I said about never entering again. I know it would make me feel better if honest artists had a real shot at winning next year."

"I'll think about it," she grumbled.

Why did I have the feeling that Malene's thinking about it would last around five seconds. As soon as I left, she'd be done.

I started heading toward the door. "Well, good seeing y'all."

As I was about to exit, Malene's phone rang. She pulled it from her purse and answered. "Hello?" Pause. "You don't say? You do say…you're kidding…how'd it happen? When was that?"

Now I was curious. The only side of Malene's conversation that I was privy to was fascinating. I had to know what it was all about.

"Sounds like a good one," Norma Ray murmured.

"Yes, we'll have some news for sure." Urleen took her foot from the sewing machine's pedal and rested it on the ground. "Sounds like a whopper of information."

"Think the Presbyterians are involved?" Norma Ray asked.

Sheesh. Really? Since when had another religious denomination become enemy number one? And what rock had I been hiding under for half my life to have missed it?

Malene spoke. "I'll be sure to keep an eye out. But if anything else happens, you let me know." She hung up and folded her arms. "Ladies, there has been a development."

"In what?" Norma Ray asked. She was basically panting, she wanted to know so badly. "Tell us!"

"In the Henrietta jewelry thief case."

"Have they found the necklace?" Urleen asked.

"You'll never guess," Malene told them.

"We won't have to if you just tell us," I snapped.

Malene scowled. "Now where is the fun in that? Half the fun of learning new information is working to get it out of me."

"Cheating scandal," was all I said.

She pursed her lips. "Fine. It turns out that since last night, Henrietta has discovered more of her jewelry gone."

Norma gasped. "No! How much?"

A sparkle that I wasn't sure I approved of lit in Malene's eyes. "All of it."

CHAPTER 7

"So someone stole all her jewelry?" Rufus asked later.

We met up for lunch at a small cafe on the far side of town. "From what I understand, yes. I don't know all the ins and outs, but according to Malene, when Henrietta got home, all her expensive jewelry had vanished."

He sat back in the booth and drummed his fingers on the tabletop. "Methinks a thief is about."

"I agree. But they must be a quick thief, because they literally stole the necklace that was around her throat and then made their way to Henrietta's house, where they acquired even more."

"Either that, or they used magic to do both."

I arched a brow. "Could we have a magical cat thief on our hands?"

"It's possible." He sipped his coffee and stared at me, the edges of his mouth curling. "If there winds up being more people who report stolen goods, we'll have to look into it. But as for now, I'd say let Tuney Sluggs do all the heavy lifting."

I nearly spit out the sweet tea that was in my mouth. "Tuney Sluggs lift anything heavy? I know you're joking."

"What would ever make you say that?" He grinned. "But I am, of course."

My mind drifted to what he had said about anyone else reporting stolen goods. What had I done with that bottle of wine? It bothered me because I knew that I had bought some pinot noir. Where had it gone? Maybe I was just becoming forgetful. What if I hadn't bought one at all —I just *thought* I had.

Perhaps I needed to start taking vitamins that enhanced memory. Which reminded me…

"Of course if Malene has anything to say about the stolen goods, I'm sure she would blame it on the Presbyterians."

He arched a brow. "The Presbyterians?"

"Apparently they don't get along with the Baptists and are akin to the devil himself."

Rufus laughed. "For some reason, when I think of evil, the word 'Presbyterian' doesn't come to mind."

"For you and me both. But there's a big rivalry in town, and Malene swears they could have their hands in anything from cheating at art competitions to…I don't know what. You name it—they'll be involved."

"Well, all of that is well and good, but I didn't ask you to lunch to discuss Malene."

"Why not? She's such a fun topic," I joked.

"As much as she is, there is something else I'd like to discuss."

"What's that?"

"Going away for a weekend—just you and me."

My jaw unhinged and nearly hit the top of the table. "Are you suggesting we embark on a getaway together?"

"That is exactly what I'm suggesting."

Wow. This was certainly a surprise. That would mean that Rufus and I would be alone, in a room, with probably only one bed. This was a HUGE step. The biggest, in fact.

Suddenly my hands were trembling. And sweating. Moisture was pouring from my pores. I wiped my palms on my jeans and hoped that he wouldn't notice.

He didn't. Rufus's gaze didn't leave my face. "What do you think? Would you like to? We could go up to the mountains or down to the beach—whatever you want."

Whatever I wanted? Well, why were we limiting ourselves? "How about an island in the Caribbean?"

"We can do that, too. But I didn't want to bring that up unless you were sure it was what you wanted." He shifted in his seat. "You see, I realized that we have very little privacy here."

What clued him in? My grandmother shouting across the street that we needed to use protection?

"So I thought," he continued, "that maybe it would be best if we got away for a bit…just a couple of days without eyes prying into your windows or animals jumping on your bed."

He was right. Lady wouldn't give us any privacy, either. My stomach quivered at the idea of being alone with him for a few days. Was that nerves? Excitement? I didn't know, and to be honest, I didn't care.

"Sure," I said. "I'd love to go away. Malene can take care of Lady. We can go whenever you want."

He took my hand. "Perfect. I'll arrange everything."

The next question hung on the edge of my tongue until it finally slipped off. "So…when do you think we'll be heading out?"

"As soon as I've got everything in place and you're able to get away from work for a few days."

I was just finishing up a barn conversion, and after that I could take a small break before my next project started.

"I'll be free in a week or so."

"Excellent," he told me with a smile. "We can go then. That gives me plenty of time to scout out the best location for us."

"I'm excited. Beach and sand and ocean—I love all those things."

"I'll love them even more because I'll be spending time with you," he confessed.

Heat flooded my cheeks. "You are too sweet."

"I try. But come on, let's finish lunch. The sooner we do that, the sooner I can begin planning."

"I can't wait."

AFTER WE ATE, I decided to get a new swimsuit. I mean, why not? If I was going to the beach with Rufus, there was no need to wear one I'd had forever. I might as well buy a new one.

There was a women's clothing boutique that also sold a few suits in the winter, so I headed there. I was nose-deep in a rack of Gstrings (not my style) when a voice behind me said, "Clem? Is that you?"

I turned to greet my grandfather. "Willard, what brings you here?"

He held a scarf in each hand. "Well, to be honest, I came in here looking for a present for Malene. I thought one of these would look good over her head when she had the top down on the Miata."

I surveyed the scarves he had picked out. One was a bright red and the other was a light pink floral pattern. "I know which one she'll like."

"The red," we said in unison before laughing.

"You got it," he agreed. "Well, I'll just put this other one back." He cupped it in his hand a minute, regarding me. "What're you doing here? Shopping for a swimsuit in January?"

Was it proper to tell my grandfather that I was planning a love weekend with my boyfriend? He might not think it very chaste of me. "Oh, just getting ahead for the summer. You know, summer bodies are made in the winter."

"They are," he said. "Well, I'd better get back to the pharmacy."

"Willard?"

"Yes?"

I paused, unsure how to broach the subject, before deciding to throw caution into the air. "What do you think of Malene's actions?" I wiggled my brows, hoping it would help Willard figure out exactly what I was talking about. "You know, about her beautiful painting."

"I'm glad you said something, Clem. Are you finished here? I'd like to talk about this outside."

I put the swimsuit back, promising myself to return and try on one that covered the butt. After Willard purchased the scarf, we stepped outside.

There was a food truck that sold pizza and pretzels pulled up to the curb. Willard rubbed his hands. "Want a soft pretzel?"

I'd just eaten, but who could turn down a soft pretzel? "Sure. No salt."

He ordered two and handed me a cup of mustard. "Let's go sit on the bench."

We did. It was a cold day. The seat of the bench was freezing, but the pretzel was warm, fresh from the oven. When I pulled it apart, steam rose from the spongy dough. "What a treat," I said.

"Isn't that right?" Willard dipped his in mustard. "But tell me what concerns you."

What *didn't* concern me? "I just wonder what you think of her using magical paints to win the contest. We haven't had a chance to discuss this, and if anyone would be against cheating, you would be. Also, if there was anyone Malene would listen to, it would also be you. Not me. She doesn't seem to care what I think."

He chuckled. "There's one thing that I learned about Malene a long time ago."

"What's that?"

"She has a mind of her own."

He glanced over at me in a knowing way, and we both laughed. "That she does," I agreed. "But still…cheating."

"I know." Willard shrugged. "If it makes you feel any better, I did try to discuss it with her. We went round and round on it for a few days, but she wouldn't budge. Nope. So I let it go. I figured, karma has a way of working itself into a person's life."

"Malene has a way of getting out of things scot-free."

"You know"—he took a bite and chewed it for a moment—"you underestimate Malene's own sense of guilt."

I laughed. "Do you think so?"

"I do. Your grandmother is a wily woman. We know that. But if you let something sit with her long enough, she'll eventually come to the right decision, make the right choice."

"I don't know. She really, really likes that ribbon, even though she can't find it."

"Sure she does. Look how people reacted to her the night she won. Malene was the star. People were congratulating and telling her that she'd done something wonderful. For an old woman, that's quite a feat." He shuffled in his seat. "You see, when you get old, people don't pay attention to you anymore. They look past you, don't see you. You're not important. All people care about is the young and beautiful, like yourself." He nudged my shoulder with his own. "Wisdom is disregarded. Age is seen as a tax instead of a benefit."

I understood what he was saying. "So when Malene won the ribbon, she was seen again."

"That's right. And it meant the world to her. I hate to take that away so quickly. Let her live in it a little. Eventually she'll come around, realize what the right thing to do is."

"You think so?"

"I *know* so." He finished his pretzel and crumpled up the wrapper. "You've just got to give her time."

"I tried to make a deal with her today."

He barked a laugh. "I would've loved to have seen that. What was this deal?"

"I said that if she never entered another art competition, I'd keep her secret."

"And what did she say?"

"I think she said that she'd think about it?" my voice rose at the end, indicating how very unsure I was at the outcome of our conversation.

He laughed harder. "You think?"

"Yeah."

Willard patted my back. "Like I said, she'll come around. Once the newness of the victory has worn off, Malene'll see that what she did was wrong. She'll probably tell Mac and Henrietta herself, and give Henrietta the ribbon she deserved all along."

"I don't know. She really dislikes those Presbyterians."

He slapped his knee. "I tell you, people always have to have something to dislike, don't they? If it's not the holiday trash pick-up schedule, it's another denomination in town."

"What's wrong with the holiday trash pick-up schedule?"

Willard shot me a coy look. "Some of us forget about holidays and put our trash out on our regular day."

"When the trash doesn't run," I said, understanding.

"Right. Then I get stuck with overflowing garbage for an entire week. But anyway, that's neither here nor there." He pointed to my wrapper. I hadn't even realized that I'd eaten all my pretzel. "You done?"

I handed it to him and rose. "Sure am."

He tossed away our trash. "Look, don't worry about Malene. She'll come around."

"Well, I'll find out soon enough. We're both supposed to hand out a meal to the needy this week. By then, I'll know exactly what's on her mind."

CHAPTER 8

The day that we were supposed to feed the needy arrived. Malene had told me to meet her at the Baptist church, which I did promptly at ten a.m. I parked right in front of Peachwood Baptist and noticed that the Presbyterian church across the street was also bustling with activity.

Malene sidled up to me. "Once a week they feed the needy, and of course, they have to make a big show of it. Huh. Putting up a big tent."

They did have a large tent erected where folks could just drive up, take a meal and go.

"Well, it seems awfully convenient," I said respectfully.

"Convenient? I don't know about that. If anything, they're trying to show us up."

I rolled my eyes. "I highly doubt that."

"Oh, do you?" she said snidely. "You don't know the Presbyterians. Look, there's Henrietta now."

In fact, there was Henrietta. She saw me across the street and waved. "I'm going to talk to her."

Malene's eyes nearly bugged from her head. "Now?"

"Yeah. Is that okay?"

"I guess." She sniffed. "But don't take long. We still have to open the kitchen and get things set up."

"I won't," I assured her. Quickly I crossed the street and waved, calling, "Henrietta!"

She smiled as I neared. "Clementine, how're you?"

"I'm okay, but I heard about what happened. How're you holding up?"

She grimaced. "Oh, those jewels that were stolen had been in my family for years—*years*. It's terrible, Clem. I never thought that anyone in our town would do such a thing." She clasped her neck as if searching for a necklace that wasn't there. "I tell you, I've never been so shocked and disappointed in my town as I have been these past days."

"I'm so sorry. Do the police have any leads?"

She shook her head. "No, they don't. No one saw anything suspicious around my house, and Tuney Sluggs spoke to everyone at the art show and even did some searching. No one had the necklace."

I patted her shoulder. "I'm sorry. But I guess as long as the Baptists weren't involved, everything should be okay, right?"

That was when Henrietta's eyes narrowed to slits. "I have been a good Christian woman all my life, but I tell you—those Baptists sometimes get my panties in a wad."

"Oh?"

"They just think they're so smart. When we started feeding the needy once a week, they went to Monday through Friday. When we had a big Easter egg hunt for the children in our town, they had to plan an even larger hunt. When we decided to have a few cars for a trunk or treat, they decided to take up their entire parking lot. Sometimes it even spilled out into the street. But did we complain? No. We did not. But I swear, they are always trying to get the best of us. And your grandmother"—she fiddled with the neckline of her sweater—"she's the worst. Now, I love Malene, and I forgive her of her transgressions, but if there was ever a woman who knew how to egg a person on, it is her."

There, I couldn't agree more. My grandmother certainly was brilliant at getting under people's skin. She was the sort of person to give you a paper cut and then pour lemon juice on it. Yes, she certainly knew how to throw gasoline on top of a fire.

I smiled kindly. "Well, keep us all posted about the jewelry, and I hope the police discover who's got it."

"Clem," Malene shouted from across the street. "We've got to get going! There's a lot of stuff to do if we're going to have the food ready before you-know-who."

By you-know-who, I was pretty sure Malene meant the Presbyterians. "Be right there," I called back.

I said goodbye to Henrietta just as Norma Ray and Urleen pulled up. Urleen had driven them, and I could see Norma Ray inside the passenger seat, clinging to the dashboard for dear life.

Urleen was only going about twenty-five miles per hour. But since Norma Ray's average speed was about five miles per hour, anything over that must've felt like she was traveling at the speed of light.

After they'd parked, Norma Ray exited and announced, "I must have an inner ear problem. It felt like we were going a hundred miles per hour."

Urleen glanced at her with hooded eyes. "Yes, you must have wonky equilibrium because we were only traveling about twenty-five."

"Is that so?" Norma Ray sounded flummoxed. "Well, I'll be."

"I'll be a henpecked egg if we don't get going," Malene snapped. "Look over there; the Presbyterians already have everything set up. We're behind, girls. We've got to get the hot dogs cooked and open the bags of chips."

"Is that what lunch is?" I asked.

Malene looked at me sharply. "Yes, why?"

"Because that doesn't exactly sound healthy. Wouldn't it have been better if we made some sort of casserole? Like, something with hearty ingredients in it?"

"I could've made a chicken poulet," Norma Ray announced. "You're right, Clem. I've been saying for years that hot dogs just won't cut it. Across the street they serve things like sausage and egg casserole. Sometimes they even make that frozen cranberry dessert."

"The one that you can put a dollop of mayonnaise on top of?" I asked.

She nodded. "That's the one."

"We don't have time to make a chicken poulet," Malene snapped. "Besides, making all that corn bread takes time."

"I don't see a shortage of Pepperidge Farm stuffing at the grocery store," Urleen said.

Malene turned crimson. "I know what I'm talking about. We're just here to hand out what's in the donation pantry, and inside there isn't cornbread dressing, chicken, and mushroom soup."

"Mm, now I'm hungry for some poulet," Norma Ray said. "When we get out of here, how about we head on over to the Freight House for some lunch? They make the best poulet."

"That sounds good," Urleen agreed. "Clem, do you think that you'd be up for that? Heading out for a bite to eat?"

Malene looked like her head was about to pop off. "Nobody is going out for lunch until we get everything fixed here. Do y'all hear me? Nobody. Now. We need to get inside and—"

"Is that peach cobbler they've got?" Norma Ray tented her eyes. "I swear, that's what it looks like. Urleen, you got your binoculars?"

Urleen rummaged through her purse. "They're in here somewhere. Oh yes. Here you go."

"Thank you." Norma Ray put the binoculars to her eyes backward. "They don't work. I can't see anything."

Malene slapped her own face. "That's because you're looking through them the wrong way."

"I knew that." Cheeks pink, Norma Ray righted the binoculars. "Oh, wow. Yes, that is quite a spread, ladies. Looks like Claire pulled that peach cobbler out from her hatchback. They're all standing around looking at it and patting her on the back for a job well done. Wait a minute. Someone's just come out of the church. She's waving her arms around. She looks really upset. She's saying something to Henrietta, and Henrietta's pointing over here, at us." Norma Ray lowered the binoculars. "Ladies, I think it's time we got inside."

But Malene was suddenly curious about all the hubbub across the street. "Why are they pointing over here? Do they look angry?" She squinted. "They do look mad. Y'all, I don't know what's going on, but we'd better run for cover."

"Let's go inside and get the lunch together." Urleen used her arms like we were cattle she was wrangling. "It might be best to not look like we're being nosy."

I agreed. So the four of us entered the church, which was terribly quiet and still. "Where're the office staff?"

"They'll be in later," Malene told me. She flipped on lights as we made our way down the hall to the kitchen. "Now, Dottie told me that everything was all set, that the hot dogs would be in the fridge along with the waters, and the chips would be in the pantry. Here we are."

Malene flipped on the lights. It was what you would expect a small church's kitchen to look like—very simple with a white refrigerator, white cabinets, a sink and a trash can. There was nothing ostentatious or flamboyant about it.

"All right, ladies," Malene said. "Y'all each grab something. I'll get the pans to serve the hot dogs in."

We spread out. I headed for the refrigerator to grab the waters and the dogs. Norma Ray followed me. I opened the door. "I'll get the heavy stuff."

"I'll let you," she told me.

But when I looked in the refrigerator, it was empty. There wasn't one hot dog. There wasn't even a crumb of food lining the shelves.

"What?" I said.

Urleen's voice rang out. "The chips aren't in here. Malene, are you sure they're supposed to be here?"

Malene, foil container in hand, marched to Urleen. "Yes, that's what she said. What the— Where are the chips?"

"And where are the hot dogs?" I moved out of the way so that both women could see inside the barren refrigerator. "There's nothing here."

"Oh goodness," Malene said, deflated. "Now what are we going to serve the needy?"

Norma Ray piped up. "Anybody got time to run to Freight House to grab some chicken poulet?"

CHAPTER 9

$\mathcal{M}$alene jumped on the phone, calling Dottie immediately. I nibbled my fingernail as she spoke.

"But there's nothing here. What do you mean, the kitchen was full when you left yesterday? Well, someone came in and stole it all. What else could've happened? I don't know who. Do you know who?" Long pause while Malene listened. "Wait. I know who it was."

She hung up without so much as a goodbye.

"Who was it?" Norma Ray said. "Who would've done such a terrible thing as to steal from a church? And God better bless whoever did this, because there is a special place in the afterlife for folks who steal from the needy."

"I thought that was folks who harmed children and the elderly," Urleen commented.

"That, too."

Malene drummed her fingers on the counter. "Who was standing around looking at us funny a minute ago? Who were all turned toward us, staring over here like baby birds with their beaks open, waiting to be fed?"

"I don't know," Norma Ray said. "I don't remember seeing any birds. Were there birds outside?"

"Not birds!" Malene dropped her voice. "The Presbyterians."

"Then why did you say birds?" Norma Ray asked, clearly lost. "I don't get it."

Malene gestured dramatically. "They looked like birds, all staring and gaping."

"If you say so."

Malene sniffed. "I do say so, and I think they're behind this."

"I don't know," Urleen said. "They looked upset about something. They didn't look as if they were happy we were about to discover that we had no food."

"We have plenty of food." Malene folded her arms and got a strange smug look on her face. "There's a whole bunch of food for us."

Norma Ray whispered to me, "What is she talking about?"

I shrugged because I didn't know, either. "What do you mean, Malene?"

She pointed toward the door. "What I mean is, those women across the street stole our food. So we're going to march on over there and steal it back."

"I don't think this is such a good idea," Norma Ray said.

"I would have to agree." Urleen shook her head. "This doesn't sound very Christian, Malene."

"They're the ones who started it. There isn't anyone more Christian than Baptists. Everybody knows that. Now. Let's get over there and reclaim what is ours."

My stomach knotted in worry. This sounded like the worst idea— ever. What was Malene going to do, charge over and demand our hot dogs back? She didn't even have proof that they had taken the church's food. My grandmother was acting on suspicion and orneriness, like she did with most things.

She was striding hard through the church, too. Before she set off World War III, perhaps it would help if I was able to calm her down. Surely she didn't want to say something that she would wind up regretting.

Oh, who was I kidding? My grandmother lived for that sort of thing.

I darted up to her. "Malene, maybe we should be calm about this. They looked upset, too. Perhaps someone stole their food."

"I doubt it," she snarled. "They're bad. They always have been, and they always will be. You'll see. We'll march right into their kitchen, and

I'm sure we'll find that they have all our goods crammed into their fridge. You just wait and see."

My stomach soured. "We should really think about this."

Malene threw open the church doors and kept right on walking. "There's nothing to think about. Now. Let's go. You need to be my backup."

"Your backup?"

"Yeah, in case someone throws a punch at me. You need to hit her back."

What? I hadn't signed up for violence. "Malene," I started but didn't get a word out before she was across the street and yelling.

"Just what do y'all think you're doing, stealing our pantry food?"

Henrietta—sweet, kind Henrietta—whirled on Malene, her brows pinched, her face rippling with fury. "Us steal your food? That's rich. We didn't steal anything. You're the ones who stole *our* food."

Malene placed her fists on her hips and jerked her head right and left as she spoke. "We didn't steal nothing. Y'all stole from us. Just how do you explain that our kitchen is completely bare?"

"Ours is, too," Henrietta snarled. "All we have to feed the needy today is peach cobbler."

"Well, that's more than us," Malene snapped. "Now. If y'all just go ahead and return the food, we'll forget all about this. We can go our separate ways."

I stood between Urleen and Norma Ray on the sidewalk. Presbyterian women (I assumed) were lining up behind Henrietta, ready to have her back. Under the small canopy sat the peach cobbler, ready to be served.

As Malene and Henrietta argued, cars pulled up. Folks stepped out of their vehicles, scratching their heads in confusion.

Those must have been the needy, the people we were all supposed to be serving the food to. If Malene and Henrietta continued to argue, we wouldn't be able to feed anyone anything. Nor would we get to the bottom of the mystery of what had happened to the food.

Time to intervene. "Ladies, it looks like we both have a problem."

"I don't have a problem," Malene said. "Because I'm the real Christian here. I didn't break into another church and steal all the hot dogs meant for those suffering and cold and hungry, unable to feed themselves."

Had I heard correctly? Was Malene actually saying that she was the better Christian when she had cheated to win an art ribbon?

"Henrietta," I said gently, "tell me what happened."

"We don't have any food and the Baptists are always trying to outdo us, so we know what happened. Right, ladies?"

The women behind Henrietta murmured "yes" and "that's right."

I could just imagine that if they had rolling pins in their hands, they would've been swinging them in a threatening manner. Good thing they didn't.

"Well, we're missing food, too. Is it possible that the same thief took both pantries?" I asked.

"They're lying," Malene said. "They're only pretending not to have food so that we don't become suspicious. As soon as we leave, they'll pull out all *our* hot dogs and serve them along with the potato chips."

"Don't forget the waters," Norma Ray added cheerfully.

Sometimes I wished she couldn't hear along with not being able to see, because mentioning the waters only added fuel to the fire.

"And the waters," Malene repeated sourly.

That did it. I could actually feel the energy in the air shift as if God himself had turned on the heater or some giant humidifier in the sky. The tension between our two groups thickened, souring.

Henrietta tightened her fists. Where had the nice lady from the art show gone?

Malene's lips dipped into a frown. That wasn't any surprise, really. I expected Malene to look more ticked as the conversation went on. But what I didn't expect was for my grandmother to march, arms swinging, over to the dessert table—the one station that housed the pan of peach cobbler.

"I don't mind if I do." Malene scooped up a spoonful of brown crust and orange congealed fruit and plopped it on a paper plate. Then she strode, still smirking, over to Henrietta and planted that plate, cobbler and all, right on her chest.

The gooey peachy dessert skidded down to her waist before dropping to the ground. It left an ugly looking smear on her nice brocade dress.

"Oh no," Urleen whispered.

"We're in for it now," Norma Ray added.

Henrietta's face was crimson. "What did you do, Malene? How could you do that? How could you ruin my dress?"

Malene scoffed. "I did it because I could and because I know that y'all are lying. You stole our food, and you deserved it."

"Why, I never." That was all Henrietta got out, because the next thing I knew, she had walked over to the cobbler, served herself up a plate, crossed back over to Malene and planted it on Malene's face like she was hitting her with a whipped cream pie.

The plate broke loose from the cobbler and drifted to the ground. Malene scooped gooey stuff from her eyes. She blinked and smiled. "You gotta do better than that if you're going to beat me, Henrietta."

That, I believe, was the turning point in the entire scene. If Malene hadn't said anything, just let everything lie, I think the entire fiasco would've been over. But because my grandmother had to get in those last words, because she couldn't allow anyone to get the best of her, the situation got out of control.

Malene dashed to the cobbler. Y'all, I'm not kidding. She didn't walk; she didn't strut. She dashed like an Olympic athlete going for gold. Scooping cobbler into the spoon, Malene hefted the long spoon over her shoulder and catapulted the dessert into the air.

It splattered onto another one of the Presbyterians. The woman shrieked. Cobbler had hit her right smack in the face, plastering the mess over her glasses. She wiped them off, headed over to the pan and launched a spoonful at Malene, who had turned back to us.

The cobbler collided with her back. Malene stood stock-still, a stony expression on her face. "Did I just get hit with cobbler?"

"You sure did," Norma Ray told her. "And it looks mighty good, too."

Urleen piped up. "I will not have Malene being the only person attacked."

"But she's the only one of us doing the attacking," Norma Ray pointed out.

"Good point," Urleen said. "Maybe we should g—"

But before she could get the word out, Urleen had been assaulted with cobbler.

Urleen, a look of horror on her face, stared down at the mess as if it was blood leaking from her chest and not a confection made of sugar and flour.

"That's it," she announced.

Next thing I knew, Urleen was catapulting cobbler into the Presbyterians. Malene joined her. Norma Ray didn't look interested in fighting until a spoonful landed on the side of her face.

Then she was in, too.

The lot of them went at it. On the Baptist side there was Malene, Urleen and Norma Ray. I hid behind a car to escape the assault. Henrietta led the charge of the Presbyterians, of which there were five women.

Clearly the Baptists were outnumbered.

"Come and help us," Malene yelled to me. "We can turn the tide, Clem. Their arthritis is starting to kick in."

She was right. Henrietta was clasping her wrist with one hand. Another woman held a tube of Aspercreme and was applying it to her knees—all while being covered in cobbler.

I figured that I could just wait it out. The one pan was nearly gone. All I had to do was just sit a few more minutes and the entire fiasco would be over. It would have to be, because those old women couldn't keep up the physical demands of hurling dessert at each other. Eventually the shoulder and knee surgeries that it appeared all of them needed would get the best of them.

As the opposing women were slowing down, Malene whispered something to Urleen and Norma Ray. They both nodded eagerly. A plan had been formed.

Yet for some reason my stomach was all queasy. Whatever they were hatching, I knew it couldn't be good. It never was when Malene was involved.

Just as Henrietta looked like she was going to concede—she had pulled a white handkerchief from her purse—Malene grabbed the pan of remaining cobbler and with Norma Ray and Urleen behind her, they charged into the Presbyterians.

The pan was up and then it came down, dumping the last of the dessert on the heads of Henrietta and her friends.

I gasped. They had gone too far. Malene had pushed the envelope and had torn it open. Henrietta would never forgive her for this. That, I was certain of.

But before my grandmother could cheer in victory, a police siren beeped. The women slowly turned—Malene and her crew looking victorious and Henrietta and her ladies drenched in dessert, looking sticky and ticked off.

Tuney Sluggs slowly made his way into the parking lot. He put the bullhorn to his lips and announced, for all the world to hear, "Ladies, put the cobbler down."

For once Malene listened.

I shook my head and sighed. What trouble were we in now?

CHAPTER 10

Juney Sluggs just gave us a warning. Though he did take a pan of cobbler with him when he left. Henrietta had apparently been hiding it, and the police chief snatched it just to make sure that no one was tempted to start the fight again, he had said.

It was embarrassing, I had to admit. But it wasn't as embarrassing as having to tell the needy families who showed up for a hot meal that we didn't have any food for them to eat.

That was the worst. Seeing the disappointment on people's faces left imprints in my mind. I resolved myself to return tomorrow with food from my own kitchen to feed them.

Malene and her cohorts were aligned with the idea as well.

"We'll come," my grandmother told me. "Just tell us when."

We made a plan, and Norma Ray added, "Is anyone going to make a cobbler? I'm suddenly hankering for some."

"No," we all answered emphatically.

She shriveled a little bit but seemed to understand. "Just thought I'd ask."

"Let's go get cleaned up," Malene said.

I followed the women back into the church. They headed for the bathroom. I didn't have to go, but I was curious if we had overlooked anything in the kitchen. Even though I knew that was impossible because we had searched the place high and low, something tickled the back of my mind. It told me to return, that I had missed something.

But what could I have missed? A lone hot dog bun? A bottle of water?

Following my instinct, I sneaked down to the kitchen and stood in the doorway. "What pulled me here?" I said aloud.

I went through every cabinet, opened every drawer once more and saw that they were all empty. Whatever my suspicion, the visit to the room had been moot. There was nothing to find in the kitchen except for a mystery that didn't look like it was going to be solved anytime soon.

No, I didn't believe that the Presbyterians had looted our church any more than I believed that the Baptists had stolen from them.

But someone had. Who? And why?

It was when I was walking back out the door that something caught my eye. Turning toward the refrigerator, I spotted a small piece of black cloth sticking like a tongue out from under the machine.

"What is that?"

Obviously, no one was going to answer. If anyone had, I was pretty sure that I would've jumped out of my skin. I was supposed to be alone, and that was how I wanted to keep things.

Since no one spoke and I did in fact, appear to be alone as I had originally believed, I picked up the scrap of black cloth. It was long, about a foot, with one end tapered to a diamond point and the other tapered to a longer diamond point.

It took a moment for me to realize exactly what I was looking at, and then it hit me—it was a tiny tie! Like one for a doll. What would a tiny tie be doing in the church's kitchen?

Before I got carried away by my imagination, I figured it must've been left there by one of the children in Sunday school. A little girl or boy probably brought their male doll with them and the tie, which was loose, fell off while they were drinking milk and eating cookies, or something.

But why hadn't I noticed it before? That bothered me. Once I spotted it, I realized it would have been nearly impossible for one of us not to have seen earlier. But then again, we'd been so frazzled looking for the food that *not* spying the tie made a lot of sense.

I crossed to the trash can and was about to throw it away when I stopped. My fingers glided over the silky material. This was good stuff. Not cheap like you'd expect. But it wasn't simply the fact that it was well-made with high-end materials that caught my attention. Buried deep in the recesses of the tie, I felt a small pulse of energy.

Magic.

Once my body tuned in to it, it was undeniable. Yes, magic raced through the tie.

Hmm. Perhaps I should hold onto it after all. So I tucked it into my jean pocket, flipped off the kitchen lights and headed back to the bathroom, where I found Malene and friends dotted from head to toe with water spots.

They looked like they'd taken a sponge bath with their clothes on. In hindsight, that was exactly what had happened.

"Well, the three of y'all look like drowned rats."

Malene flicked water from her hands. "I *feel* like a drowned rat. But anyway, we got the Presbies."

Presbies? Now they had a nickname for the church across the street? Sheesh.

"I'm not sure we got them," Norma Ray added. "It seems like it was sort of a draw."

Urleen said in a surly voice, "After all, when the police show up, it's never a good sign that anyone won."

"We won," Malene said emphatically. "We won and don't y'all forget it. Now. Let's come up with a game plan for tomorrow."

The game plan, as it turned out, required me to make the hot dogs and bring the waters as they were too heavy for the women to carry. Norma Ray would bring the potato chips. Urleen would make potato salad, and Malene would bring a cobbler or two. Just in case, she had said.

"Just in case of what?"

She scowled. "In case we need to be ready for battle."

I rolled my eyes. "How about for now we just go home and get ready for tomorrow?"

Malene smiled like a snake. "Yes, why don't we?"

WHEN I ARRIVED HOME, Lady gave me a good once-over. "I'm starving! Where have you been?"

"Oh, it's been a day. Malene got into a food fight with some old ladies."

Lady licked her chops. "Don't torture me! I cain't hear one more thing about food. Make me some grub, now!"

I laughed and poured her a bowl of food. "Here you go."

She ate a bit, but the whole time she had a funny look on her face. "What's that in your pocket?"

"What're you talking about?"

"That magic. You got magic in that pocket."

When had my dog been able to sense power like that? "You can tell?"

"What do you think? My nose don't work? I am a canine, Clem. I can smell things, and magic is one of them."

"Okay, okay. Just as long as you don't start seeing ghosts and barking at them, we're all good."

"Oh, you mean like that man who lives in your bedroom?"

"What!?"

She laughed. "I'm just joshing you. There ain't no man in your bedroom."

"Whew."

"He lives in the bathroom."

"What?" My hair stood on end. "Please tell me that you're joking."

"I am."

Relieved, I sat on a chair and pulled the tie from my pocket. "I found this in the church kitchen after the food disappeared."

Kibble dropped from her mouth as she said, "Tell me everything."

So I did, leaving nothing out. When I was done, Lady padded over to sniff the tie. "It smells funny. I ain't never smelled some kind of scent like that, and I don't like it. You'd better get rid of it."

"No. It's a clue."

"I smell death and destruction with it."

I shook my head. "There's no way that you can smell death and destruction from one tie."

My dog lifted her nose in the air. "Okay. Whatever you say. But I'm telling you that nothing good will come of you keeping it."

She was sweet, but Lady was prone to dramatics. "I think you're overreacting."

"You just wait and see. I'm right. I know it."

There was something so matter-of-fact in the way she said it that made me question myself. What if Lady was right? What if keeping hold of this tiny tie with magic was a bad idea?

But whatever had created this tie had stolen from the church. The culprit had to be found. They had to be discovered and brought to justice. It wouldn't be right just to let something like that slide.

So even though my stomach rolled and a teensy voice inside my head told me that perhaps it would be best to get rid of the tie, I decided to keep it.

"You ain't gonna get rid of it, are you?" my dog said as if sensing my thoughts.

"I'm not."

"Well, don't you come crying to me when I say I told you so."

Her haughty attitude made me laugh. "Why not?"

"Because I'm gonna be busy washing my hair and snuggling up to my stepdaddy."

I groaned. "Please don't call him that in front of me."

"Why not? The sooner he figures out that's his role, the sooner he'll take to the idea." Her eyes filled with whimsy. "I can just see it—he'll take me for walks in the park, we'll play Frisbee, he'll let me lick the ice cream off his cone."

"Ice cream isn't good for dogs."

"Says you."

Tired of being put in my place by Lady, I rose. "Come on. Let's go shopping."

Her tail swept back and forth in excitement. "What're we shopping for?"

"Hot dogs and water."

"Sounds like dinner to me."

The Foodland down the road didn't mind me bringing Lady in. Well, that wasn't exactly true. I usually smuggled her in a big purse and let her sit in the children's chair seat on top of the buggy. Soon as she was in position, Lady's nose was out and working in overdrive.

"Oh, I want it all, Clem. Will you get me some of that doggy peanut butter ice cream?"

"If you're good."

"I'll be good."

We loaded up on hot dogs and water, filling the buggy nearly to the top. People stared at my cart, and I just smiled. They must've thought that I was doing my monthly shopping and lived on a strict diet of processed meat and purified tap water.

We paid and left, heading home. It was getting late, and I fixed us some supper. Rufus called me, and we chatted for a few minutes, making plans to meet up the next day. I didn't mention the tie because frankly, I forgot about it. But when I was going to bed, I pulled it from my pocket and stared at it, wondering what secrets it held.

At first I dropped it on my nightstand, but remembering Lady's warning, instead I stowed it in my closet with the golden hammer that wreaked as much damage as it did good.

When everything was safely tucked away and my face was scrubbed to shining, I curled up with Lady in my bed and told her good night.

The next day, dawn broke brightly through my blinds. The sun was already splashing pinks and yellows on my walls by the time I stretched, ready to face the day.

I padded sleepily into the kitchen to make coffee, all the while ignoring Lady's blathering about her breakfast. Coffee first. My dog was not going to starve, no matter how much she wanted me to think so.

I dumped grounds in the dispenser and placed a mug under the Keurig. With my eyes still slitted, I opened the fridge to grab the creamer and stopped.

Stared.

Could not believe my eyes.

All the hot dogs I had bought yesterday, including the water and everything else that had been in my refrigerator the night before, was gone.

Missing.

Someone or something had sneaked into my house and stolen the goods right out from under my nose.

CHAPTER 11

"Lady, come here!"

My dog hightailed it into the kitchen. "What is it, Clem? Is there a fire? No, there ain't a fire. I'd smell it if there was one."

I gestured to the inside of my refrigerator. "It's all gone—the hot dogs, the water. It's vanished."

She stared, shocked. Then after a moment my dog murmured, "I knew that you'd sleep eaten before, but nothing like this. What did you do, Clem?" Her gaze scanned me from top to bottom. "And where could you have hidden all that food? Your stomach ain't even big."

I shut the fridge door. "I'll have you know that I did not eat this. I don't sleep-eat."

Lady lifted her nose to the air. "That's what they all say."

"I don't."

"Sure. But if you don't, then what happened to that last fried chicken leg last week? Remember when you woke up and it was gone?"

She was right. Maybe I did sleep-eat. Yet this was the not the time to be concerned about my nighttime habits. "Well, even if I did eat a chicken leg—"

"You did."

"Even *if* I did, I did not eat an entire refrigerator full of hot dogs and drink a bunch of waters."

"Are you sure about that?"

"Yes, I'm sure. I would know if—"

"*Hehehehe.*"

We both froze. Lady's eyes widened. The fear and worry in them was palpable. My own heart rate had ticked up to about a thousand beats a minute. I hated to ask the question, but one of us needed to.

"Did I hear what I think I heard?"

"A small giggle coming from somewhere in this house?" she whispered. "Yes, I think so."

"You're a dog. Go sniff it out."

She reeled back. "I might be a dog, but I'm tiny. I ain't no German shepherd. You want a real dog in a fight. I'm just around to look pretty."

"I'm very disappointed in you."

"You can be all the disappointed you like," she said with a scoff. "That don't change nothing. I'm a lap dog."

"For whose lap? You're really long, in case you haven't noticed."

"I resent that remark. But because I love you, I will ignore it and not hold it against you."

"Hehehehe."

I grabbed an iron skillet from atop the stove and hoisted it over one shoulder. There was someone or something in my house, and it was laughing.

I was so afraid that I thought I might vomit. Really. My stomach was twisting and churning. Bile had already surged up the back of my throat once, burning it. Or maybe that was heartburn. Either way, I was in a state of worry.

But seeing as how Lady was not going to actually help me in this situation, I took a slight step forward. "Get behind me. I'll protect you."

"Oh, thank goodness. You are my knight in shining armor."

"Don't push it," I told her. "Just do as I say. You may have to run across the street."

"To safety, I understand. One of us has to make it out alive." She shook her head. "I'm sorry that you're going to sacrifice yourself for me. But your death won't be in vain. I'll place flowers on your grave every week."

"Come on. That's not going to happen. All I meant was for you to go over to Malene's and have her send Willard over, or call Rufus."

"Oh." She suddenly looked very guilty. "Right. I knew that was what you meant."

Sure you did. "Now. Do as I said and get behind me."

We made our way slowly from the kitchen into the living room. I hadn't heard the giggle again, but I figured it wasn't gone. It had wanted me to know that it was there. That was why it had giggled in the first place.

I decided to speak to it, see if we could come to an agreement. "Hello? Whoever you are, I know that you took my hot dogs." And now I suspected that it had taken the hot dogs from the church as well. "Can you please give them back? They're for the needy in town. I would be happy to make you a meal. You don't have to steal from me. All you have to do is ask and I'll help you."

I waited, but there wasn't a reply except for Lady nudging my calf with her nose. "That was good, Clem. Even I would've given the dogs back to you after that speech."

Yeah, right after she ran from the house and left me for dead.

Perhaps Lady wasn't getting enough love from me. No way. All I did was snuggle with her and tell her how much I loved her. Maybe a dog's true loyalty was to him- or herself.

No. That didn't seem right, either.

Perhaps the answer was that my dog was selfish, plain and simple.

Yep. That sounded more like it.

"Maybe it's gone," Lady whispered.

"Hehehehe."

I jumped. The sound had come directly from my right. I whirled toward it, skillet raised in a weapon-holding stance.

"Who's there?" I said.

But the space was empty. There was nothing standing to my right. Nothing to my left. Whatever I was dealing with, it enjoyed tricking me. It liked getting my panties in a knot and frazzling me to a tizzy.

"I'm out," Lady shouted, rushing toward the door. "I ain't gonna stay in no house with a disemboweled voice."

"It's *disembodied* voice."

"Well, whatever it is, I ain't staying. Let me out!"

I opened the door. "Go to Malene's."

"I'm on it."

My dog dashed off my porch as fast as greased lightning. Huh. I wondered why I couldn't get her to move that fast on a regular day.

But with Lady gone, that meant I didn't have to worry about her safety. I only had myself to be concerned with. "Can we talk?" I said to the walls. "You obviously want me to know that you're still here. So let's have a conversation. Let's chat about things."

Was I supposed to start with the obvious—*I know you're hurting inside? What could be bothering you? Were you abandoned when you were young? Did you not get enough love from your parents? Do you simply need a hug?*

Maybe when I came face-to-face with whoever this was, I could go there. But not until then.

"Hehehehe," came the voice.

And then a vase lifted into the air by an invisible hand and was tossed against my mantel, where it crashed against the brick and smashed into bits.

"Why, you!" I shouted, not sure what else to do. How could I fight something that I couldn't see? What was I supposed to do?

My mind kicked into overdrive, and apparently so did my body. I started swinging the skillet through the air, hoping to randomly hit the perpetrator in my home. It was a foolish thing to do. Not only was the skillet heavy (I really should've traded it out for a broom), but there was no way for me to know where the creature was.

"Hehehehe," taunted the voice.

"Listen," I said, breathless from my aerobic workout, "I was trying to be nice. I wanted to discuss our problems as adults. In fact, I don't even have a problem with you. I'm not upset. Well, I am a little now because you smashed one of my possessions. But all I wanted to do was chat things through. But now you've done it. You're going to make me bring out the big guns. You won't like it. You'd better go before something bad happens to you."

Wow. Was I blowing steam or what? The only thing I could hope was that the creature didn't know how full of hot air that I really was.

But all I got in response was a picture frame tossed and broken against my mantel.

"Would you stop that?" I screeched.

The bodiless laugh rang in my ear again. My blood pressure was up now. My palms were sweating. I was angry but also smart enough to realize that I was in over my head. I had no way to fight this creature. It controlled all the cards. If I was going to beat it at its own game, I had to play smarter—a lot smarter.

I had to go all psychological warfare on its butt.

No problem. I could do that.

Couldn't I?

"I have something of yours."

I felt it—a shift in the air. It was instantaneous. As if the creature had filled the very atmosphere with its mischief and mayhem. But once I cut its foot off, the thing sobered up. And so did the room.

"You'll want it back," I told it, knowing that I had its attention. "But the only way that I'll give it to you is if you stop and return everything that you've taken."

At that point I had the feeling that the creature had taken a lot more than food. I suspected Henrietta's jewels might have been in its possession as well. Goodness knew what else the little perpetrator had stolen.

The calm in the air shifted. It was palpable and so electric that it surprised me that my hair didn't stand on end.

I wasn't sure exactly what the change meant. Was the creature going to be nice? Was it going to stop laughing and take the time to speak with me?

Surely that's what it would do. If it had any sense at all, the thing would know that it was best to be nice, play together, all that good stuff.

"Well? Would you like to talk this out? Do you want back what's yours?"

Nothing happened for a good long minute, and then a glass paperweight on a side table lifted and hurled to the hearth. The object had been a gift to myself, something that I'd seen at a yard sale on the side of the road. I'd bought it as a reward for landing my first renovation job.

Now it was smashed against the brick. Bits of glass stuck to the hearth, making it glint like diamonds.

I was ticked.

I curled my one free hand into a fist. "That was an antique."

"Hehehehe."

I shoved up the sleeves of my pajamas. "Okay. Whatever you are, this means war."

Books were pulled from a bookshelf and tossed toward me. There was no way that I'd ever win against this thing unless I could see it.

An idea popped into my head. I raced into the kitchen and grabbed a sack of flour from the cupboard. I might not have cooked a whole lot, but I always kept staples in the house in case the urge to bake every overcame me.

That happened a lot during the holidays. I'd watch a few episodes of *The Great British Baking Show,* and the next thing I knew, I thought that I was Paul Hollywood and could bake some sort of crazy bread stuffed with nuts and meat.

No, my creations never turned out as good-looking as his, but they were usually edible. So I considered that a win.

Carrying the skillet and the flour, I raced back to the living room. My house was slowly but surely being torn apart. I laid the skillet on the couch and waited for the little terrorizing freak to strike again.

Turned out, I didn't have to wait long. Less than thirty seconds later, a lamp lifted from a table. Except for the shade and bulb, that lamp was an antique and made of colored glass.

There was no way that I was going to let the little dweeb destroy it.

I flung my hand in the flour, pulled out a fistful and threw it by the lamp. The white powder floated down and did exactly what I had hoped—it outlined the creature.

Now I could see it.

It was small, about a foot and a half tall. I couldn't make out much else, though. Just the shape that the flour defined.

I raced to the lamp and yanked it from its grasp. "No, you don't!"

The creature let go and scampered back over to the bookcase. I followed it and at the same time wished that instead of the skillet in my hand, that I had a sack. Then I could toss it over the creature.

But anyway, without the sack, all I could do was scare it. It grabbed a book, and I yanked it away.

The creature froze for a blink. Then it lifted its arms. A lightbulb went on inside its head, I was sure of it. It now knew that I could see it.

"You can't run from me," I said. "Now, let's talk."

"Hehehehe!"

I really hated this thing.

The little monster raced to my couch and had pulled off a cushion when the front door opened.

Rufus stepped inside. The wind picked up his hair and the long duster-like jacket he wore, making it ripple.

Like, was this a movie set? How was it that he could make such a dramatic entrance?

He spotted the flour-covered critter, raised his hand and said, *"Relinquo!"*

A cloud of smoke engulfed the creature. It popped and fizzled, and when I opened my eyes, the creature was gone.

Rufus's gaze darted to me. "Are you okay?"

I rushed to him. "Yes. I'm fine. But what was that thing?"

"That," Rufus said darkly, "was a sprite, and I'm afraid it only does one thing."

"What's that?"

His jaw clenched. "It turns the world upside down."

CHAPTER 12

"So are you saying it wreaks havoc?" I asked a little while later. Rufus had helped me clean up the mess in my house, and then we'd headed over to Malene's, where Lady was waiting for us.

Lady, to her credit, had done exactly as I had asked. She had rushed over to Malene's, told her to call Rufus and had stayed there. The whole while my dog had gotten stroked by Malene and fed bacon. Apparently Lady had whined to my grandmother that I never gave her anything good to eat and that she was starving.

Sheesh. What a dog.

"Sprites brings bad things," Malene answered for Rufus.

I didn't hide my surprise. "And you know this how?"

"Because I've had my experiences with sprites before. I should've known that one was behind all the stealing."

"Instead you decided to blame the Presbyterians," I told her.

She shrugged. Clearly she didn't care that she had cast the first stone at a bunch of innocent old ladies.

"I've dealt with them too," Rufus ground out. "They're not fun. Not in the least. They wreak havoc unless you can catch them. Which they tend to make impossible."

"Impossible? Nothing's impossible," I argued.

Willard entered with a tray of coffee and doughnuts. "Clem? Rufus? Help yourselves."

I fixed coffee for both of us and snagged a chocolate doughnut. What? I hadn't eaten breakfast yet. Malene and Willard were lucky that I was even dressed. I'd almost forgotten to change out of my pajamas before Rufus pointed it out to me.

But anyway, being dressed and finally getting caffeinated and fed helped my mood. I wasn't agitated from the attack on my house anymore. Okay, I was a little. But distance and time healed all wounds, and my wounds were sewing up fast.

Except when it came to the mysterious sprite part. I glanced from Rufus to Malene. "Okay, who wants to tell the story?"

"What story?" Willard asked.

"The sprite one," Malene told him.

"Oh." He wrung his hands. "Not a good tale."

Now my interest was piqued even more. Malene gave his elbow a gentle push. "Why don't you spin the yarn?"

"Okay. Let me think." Willard sipped his coffee and took a bite of doughnut. Lady padded over to his feet and stared up at him, waiting for a crumb, any crumb to drop into her jaws. "Well, I'd say it happened about twenty years ago."

"Eighteen," Malene corrected.

"Do *you* want to tell the story?" he asked bluntly.

"No, no. You do it. You say it better than I do, anyway."

"Go on," I said to Willard.

For goodness' sake, I'd never hear the story if Willard and Malene didn't stop fighting over who was going to have the right to tell it. *Just get on with it,* I nearly shouted.

Willard spoke. "Eighteen years ago, Peachwood had what some would call an infestation of sprites. Some kids found a way to conjure them. Now, it's one thing to conjure one sprite, quite another to call up an entire village."

"You've got to be joking," Rufus said sternly. "An entire village of sprites descended here?"

"You got it." Willard took another bite of food and spoke between chews. "At first, little things happened like the fountain outside the big bank got shut off. No plumber or city worker could find anything wrong with it. But when it started spewing green goo, we knew that this wasn't any sort of normal situation."

"It was bad," Malene said sadly.

"The green sludge was our first clue," Willard confessed. "But we still didn't know the source of the culprits until one night all heck broke loose."

"What happened?" I asked.

"I tell you, if we had thought the fountain was the worst of it, we were wrong. Traffic lights exploded, which led to dozens of car accidents. Store windows were smashed in. The appliance store down the street was broken into. All the guts from the refrigerators and stoves were yanked from their housing and threaded together. The appliances were turned on, and it created a power surge that cast Peachwood in darkness. And that was when the worst began."

"It got worse?" It was hard to believe anything could've been worse than that. But it must have, because neither Willard nor Malene had ever bothered to tell me this story before. That could only have meant one thing—things got so bad that they wanted to forget all about them. A knot formed in my throat at that singular thought. I swallowed it back down. "How much worse?"

Willard and Malene exchanged a sobering glance that sent a shiver straight down my spine.

Oh, that bad, huh?

Willard's gaze dropped to his hands. When he lifted it back to me, his eyes were damp. Was he about to cry?

"It's hard to talk about," he explained. "It's a dark part of our history, one that many of us would rather forget."

"All of us," Malene said.

"Okay, all of us. Whereas one sprite might have been more of a prankster, they all hold a bit of unbridled mischief inside them. They're a little violent but should be, for the most part, harmless."

"I'm sorry, how does being only a teensy bit violent marry with the idea of being harmless?" I asked, now totally confused. "The one in my house was smashing glass against my hearth."

Willard clapped his hands. "That's what I'm saying. That should be the extent of how uncontrolled they'll act—breaking a few things. At least, that's how it is when they're alone."

"They think it's funny," Rufus added.

Ah, now I got it. The sprite had been laughing the entire time. It liked having my goat. The idea of besting me amused it. "Now I understand."

Willard nodded. "Yes, well, that's if you only have one sprite that you're dealing with. But when there's a larger number, their mischievous ways tend to multiply, get out of control. That's what happened here. When the village of sprites were called down on us, they started destroying property, wreaking havoc. But that was the easiest part of it. Not long after, their pranks turned deadly."

His words were a punch to the chest. My lungs squeezed, and it took a moment before I could suck a breath back down. "Deadly?"

He gave a slight nod as if completely admitting the truth would somehow hurt him. "The first person who died was old Mrs. Whitlock. She was a nasty sort, the kind that when kids accidentally knocked a ball in her yard, she would keep it. It was winter and below freezing. The sprites spilled water all down her front steps and walkway. Mrs. Whitlock slipped and being old, broke her back. She never recovered."

"Then they got their hands on that car," Malene reminded him.

"Oh, right." Willard rubbed a hand down his tired face. "They hotwired a vehicle, got behind the wheel and plowed into a crowd of people. Two died, I believe."

He looked to Malene for confirmation and she nodded. "This was only in one night," my grandmother explained. "By the end of our ordeal, at least two more were dead."

Good grief, those sprites were evil, terrible creatures. The lot of them needed to be locked up in jail, the key thrown away forever.

"There were more?" I asked in disbelief.

"By that time, some of us figured out what was going on," Willard said. "Malene and I were two of them. We rounded up our friends, those with magic and without, and we went after the sprites, capturing and banishing them. It took all night to find them and get rid of every last one. But we managed." His voice broke when he added, "I just wished we'd done it sooner, to save some of those lives."

Malene patted his shoulder. "We did the best we could."

Even though they were obviously still tortured by this, I considered it great news. From the way Willard told it, getting rid of the sprites had been easy. All they'd had to do was some banishing or something.

"Y'all have to look on the bright side. You got rid of the sprites. You were able to defeat them, and you had an entire village to deal with. We've only got one. Granted, I don't know where it is."

I glanced at Rufus, and he replied, "I only sent it from your house. I don't know where it went to."

"Okay, so we don't have an exact location, but we can get one. That should be no problem. It probably didn't go far, and I'm sure someone will report their pantry being hacked into and all the food stolen. In fact, we should put out posters, telling people to call us if that happens. That way, we'll be on top of the situation. We can beat this little guy, I know it."

I smiled widely. In fact, I could feel myself beaming all the way to my toes. This problem was almost solved, like ninety-eight percent solved. All we had to do was find the creepy little creature and send it back to where it had come from. Easy-peasy lemon squeezy.

We so had this.

"There's one problem," Rufus said.

Great. He had to say it, didn't he? He had to find one problem. Why couldn't he have said, there was a small complication instead of using the word 'problem'?

"What's that?" I asked.

He raked his fingers through his dark tresses. "What Willard hasn't said yet is *how* they got rid of the sprites."

All gazes swiveled to my grandfather. "Oh, right," he admitted. "I haven't discussed that. I made it sound easy to get rid of the little buggers."

"Well, wasn't it?" I asked, my heart jumping into my throat.

"We first had to locate the people who'd called the sprite. That wasn't too hard because they were in the thick of the mess. Once we were able to do that, Malene asked what spell they'd used to call the creatures."

"They'd used several orbs," she explained, "as well as an old chant."

I could feel my face heating up. My blood pressure was skyrocketing under all the stress of this conversation. "And what did you do?"

"We had to perform the chant backward, that was the key. It took some time to figure out, but once we had that, the rest was easy."

I brushed my hands as if cleaning them of dirt. "So this is still no problem. We get that chant, find the sprite and send him home. Done."

Malene shook her head sadly. "My dear, what I'm afraid no one is saying is that we don't know what spell called the creature. We don't know what magic brought it here. It is a magical being and can't simply be banished with any magic because it has its own power to counteract anything we do. In order to successfully get rid of it, we need to know who called it, why and how. Those are the three keys. Until we have that knowledge, we're acting blindly, unable to see the forest for the trees."

Was she using that term correctly? I didn't know, but it mattered little. What my grandmother was telling me was that until we understood the root cause of the problem, we would have a pantry prankster on our hands indefinitely.

"So," Rufus said stoically, "you understand the depth of our problem. Just one sprite, we can handle. But if more are called, a lot more, then…"

His voice trailed off, but I knew what he was thinking. If more sprites were called, our town, our population was doomed.

CHAPTER 13

"So how bad is it?" I asked Rufus sometime later. We were outside, walking down the street. Lady was on her leash, leading the way, which was how she liked things—to be in charge, I mean.

I'm sure that surprises y'all.

Sarcasm definitely included in that last comment.

Rufus punched his fists into his pockets. "How bad is it? I don't know yet. I wish that I did. I wish that I could say I had all the answers. But I don't. I don't know how to find something that we can't see. I could summon it but not banish it."

His brow pinched, and I realized that Rufus was worried. Now, I had definitely seen him be concerned before. That was a given. But there was something about the sprite that rattled him. It made me wonder if I should have been disturbed as well.

"What's bothering you?"

"Nothing. Everything."

"That's quite a rainbow of fruity flavors."

He chuckled. "There's really nothing rainbowlike about it. It's a mess of darkness, actually."

"Tell me."

He shot me a furtive glance and exhaled. "I suppose that first and foremost, I'm worried about you. I have no way of keeping the sprite out of your house. It knows where you live. It knows that I sent it away, though temporarily. My biggest fear—well, I shouldn't say 'fear.' My biggest concern is that the creature will return and its pranks could get out of control."

I scoffed. "And attempting to destroy all my house on a hearth *isn't* getting out of control?"

"I'm afraid it would do worse. Something that could cause real damage, like rewiring your toaster, which might result in a fire—that sort of thing."

A fire? What if I was asleep? What if I slept through the smoke alarm? What if? *What if?* I shouldn't have dragged Rufus into this conversation. Now I felt worse than I had before. Before, I was just thinking that the sprite would cause death and destruction only if an army was with it. But now I could see how one simple prank could become deadly.

I hugged my waist. "I wish that I'd never brought up the subject."

"I'm sorry. I didn't mean to worry you."

Lady glanced back at us. "You won't be worrying her if you spend the night. But no hanky-panky. My hearing is exceptional. So is my sense of smell. Don't make me spell out for you what that means. Just keep your hands to yourselves."

Rufus's cheeks turned pink. *Way to go, Lady. Embarrass your stepdaddy. That'll make him stay around.*

I took hold of his wrist. "What should we do? About the sprite, I mean?"

The red on his cheeks melted away. "First and foremost, we find out who called the creature."

"How?"

"That, I don't know. It's the biggest problem we have and the most important one to solve. Without that knowledge, we're working blind. And as for your situation..."

"Yes? What about me? If we can't keep the sprite out, what are we supposed to do?"

He rubbed his chin in thought. Then, ever so slowly, a sparkle twinkled in his eyes. "If we can't keep the creature out, perhaps we make it unbearable for him to be in your house."

"I'm not following."

"I ain't either," Lady called.

Gosh, Lady heard everything and commented on all of it. It made me wish that I could communicate with Rufus telepathically. That way, Lady wouldn't be privy to every single detail of information that escaped my lips or his.

Rufus, however, had no idea of what I was thinking, because he started explaining his plan. At first I was skeptical, but the more I listened, the more I liked it. It was good, great really—a winner winner chicken dinner of an idea.

The only thing was, I wasn't sure if we could pull it off.

"What do you think?" he asked after he'd told me everything.

I considered it, studied the unbridled exuberance in his eyes. This was Rufus's way of protecting me. I knew that. I needed to let him know that I appreciated it.

I smiled. "Well, all we can do is try."

He rubbed his hands. "Great. I say we get started."

So soon? "Now?"

He nodded. "Now."

~

"WE ARE GOING to make your home one big booby trap," Rufus explained.

"We're going to plant a huge pair of boobies in here? Whose boobies are they gonna be?" Lady glanced at me in surprise. "Yours? Your pair ain't big enough."

Talk about embarrassing. "Um. No. That's not what Rufus means."

"Well, someone needs to explain it to me and fast, because I ain't gonna stay in a house with bodiless boobies."

That time, I barked a laugh. "What he means is—we're going to plant traps all over the home."

Her eyes narrowed. "I hope not the kind that'll hurt me."

Rufus knelt in front of her. "Nothing that I do will harm you, Lady. I promise."

"If you say so." She paused a moment. "Okay. How're we gonna go about this?"

"*You* are going to stay out of them," I told her. "That's how this will go. You're going to watch and make sure you keep far, far away from any and all traps."

"Don't I at least get to set one?"

She looked so hopeful, her big sad puppy-dog eyes on full display, that I hated to say no. "Okay. You can help."

"Yay!"

I smiled at Rufus. "All right. Lead the way."

"I don't mind if I do."

After we got my house nicely booby-trapped, Rufus and I made plans for later, and I set out to walk around downtown. I was tired and my nerves were still frazzled from what had happened first thing that morning. There was nothing like waking up to a giggling intruder to really set you on edge.

Malene had called the church pastor that morning and explained that once again, we wouldn't have hot dogs for the needy. Luckily the pastor said his wife had been baking casseroles and storing them away for later Sunday dinners, so he said they could cook up a few of those and serve them. Malene offered for her, Urleen and Norma Ray to dish up the food. Since I'd been traumatized, my grandmother told me that I could take the day off.

And what I needed was retail therapy. I didn't necessarily need to buy anything, but just shopping around made me happy. I loved that. So the first place I went to was Architectural Scavengers. Yes, I realized that most girls went clothes shopping when they needed a pick-me-up. Not me. I preferred to be surrounded by old house hardware and finishes, chandeliers, mantels and cast-iron tubs.

Yes, I was weird. I was happy to admit that.

As soon as I entered, Lance Dewald greeted me with air-kisses to both cheeks. "Clementine, darling. It's been much too long since we last saw one another. Here." He walked me over to an antique horsehair chair. "Sit. Tell me everything. Is the reason I haven't seen you because you've found the love of your life?"

I laughed. "Hardly. I've been so busy with…"

"Magic?" he asked, eyebrows wagging.

"Yes, I suppose you could say that. But not mine."

"Oh, honey. Tell me about it. Things in town are changing. People who never had magic before are coming into it. It's strange and fun, I guess."

"What do you mean?"

Lance smoothed his hair. "Well, I suppose what I mean is that I've seen people working spells. I saw a woman standing right beside a blender in a department store. Next thing I knew, the blender was on, its blades whirling at high speed. Here's the thing—it wasn't plugged in. There's so much magic here, it's like the very air is now energized with it."

Just then, Patrick, Lance's partner in business and love, entered. Patrick's chocolate-brown eyes landed on Lance, and he shook his head. "Dear, are you giving Clementine an earful of things she doesn't need to hear?"

"Oh, I need to hear them," I countered.

Patrick laughed. "If you say so." To Lance he added, "Before you get too carried away, don't forget that I need help unpacking those glass sconces."

"Glass sconces?" I couldn't help but to butt my nose into their business. "Now you're speaking my language."

"Oh, they're gorgeous," Lance gushed. "Came from a nineteenth-century home up East. The family was selling everything to renovate, and we got these. They used to cover up the gas lights that lined the wall. They're gorgeous. I'll show them to you."

"Yes, please."

Lance blew Patrick an air-kiss. "I'll be right back."

I followed Lance to the back where an unopened crate lay on the ground. He grabbed a crowbar and pried the lid off. Buried under what seemed like enough hay to fill a barn, lay the sconces.

They were gorgeous, teardrop shaped with a cut-crystal rim at the top. "Wow." I whistled. "These are nice. How much do you want for them?"

Lance balked. "You don't even know how many there are."

"I don't. But I'm sure that I'll have a job soon enough where I can use them. How much?"

He named a price, and I shot back another. I couldn't just go with Lance's first offer, and *he* knew that I couldn't, either. We had been friends long enough to know that bartering was a part of that relationship.

When we did agree on a price, we shook on it, and I pulled out my debit card and handed it to him. While he was writing up the paperwork, I perused the store some more. More folks had wandered in. I spotted Mac from the art show. He waved. I returned it.

I also saw Jessica shopping in the knobs section. I headed over. "Hey, there."

She looked surprised to see me but quickly righted her expression and demurely tucked a strand of hair behind one ear. "Hey, Clem. How're you?"

"I'm…good." I was good. It wasn't a lie. Okay, so it wasn't exactly the truth what with the whole sprite thing going on, but I was going to stick as close to the truth as possible. "How're you?"

"Good. Great." She grinned, revealing a row of straight, white teeth. "I've been settling into town."

The way she said it, even though she smiled, I had the feeling that Jessica was lonely. "Hey, I'd love to have lunch with you sometime."

Her smile brightened. "You would?"

"Absolutely. If I'm on a job, I can usually sneak away, no problem. It'd be great to hang out if you're available."

"Yeah. I'm usually free. That sounds good." Her smile suddenly faltered. "Do you know if they ever found out what happened to Henrietta's jewels?"

"No, I don't think so." But I suspected a small sprite was behind the fiasco. "Hopefully they will soon, though."

"Yeah, I hope so." Her gaze dropped to the ground for a moment before darting back to my face. "Okay, well. When would you like to have lunch?"

We made plans to meet the next day, at a small cafe downtown. By that point, loads of people were milling into Architectural Scavengers. I'd never seen the place so busy, but Lance and Patrick had a penchant for selling really stellar stuff, hence the sconces I was about to purchase.

Lance packed them into the back of my truck for me. I thanked him and was about to leave when Mac, the art show curator, waved me down.

"Clem," he called. "Wait up!"

He was wearing floral Bermuda shorts and a short-sleeved T-shirt. Some people, no matter how cold it got in the South, refused to wear appropriate clothing for winter. You'd never see anything like that up North. But in the South, it was a whole "thing."

"Hey, Mac. Everything okay?"

He shook his head. His blond hair flapped against his forehead. I was afraid that if the wind picked up, it might snatch the flap right off the top of his head.

"No," he said tartly. "Everything is not okay."

"Why not?"

"Because." Mac's eyes narrowed. "I know that Malene lied."

CHAPTER 14

Oh no. Mac knew that Malene had used magical paints to create her winning portrait. What would he do? Would he strip her of her ribbon that she'd lost? Would he tell the entire town? Would he shame her so badly that the residents of Peachwood banished her into the wilderness?

Wait. Perhaps I should have taken a moment to get ahold of myself.

This was what I wanted, wasn't it? I wanted Malene to pay for the wrong that she had done. I wanted her to admit that she had lied and return the award that wasn't hers to begin with. It should have been Henrietta's.

So Mac was doing me a favor. Wasn't he?

Surely he was.

So instead of freaking out, I simply replied, "Yes. I know. I'm so sorry."

He blinked. "Sorry? Why're you sorry?"

Um. Was he kidding? "It's so completely unprofessional, and I told her not to do it."

He clapped my shoulder. "It's not bad at all. It's wonderful!"

"I'm sorry. But are we talking about the same thing?"

He chuckled. Actually touched his belly and laughed. Who did that?

This guy, that was who. "I'm talking about the fact that Malene lied and said that she couldn't paint."

"Oh, okay. When did she say that?"

"She's always said it. Your grandmother is the humblest person I've ever met."

"Humble. Right."

I did not hide the sarcasm in my voice, but he replied, "She is. Malene is about as humble as they get. But perhaps she'd never quite had the right subject before." He winked at me. "I think painting you did something to her. It brought out the true brilliance in her work. She was able to see you, her granddaughter, and turn you into the piece of art that you are."

Okay, this conversation was not going the way that I had expected, or wanted. How to get out of it before it got creepy weird? Because that was the direction I could sense it was headed toward.

"Thank you for saying that, and I will be sure to tell Malene that you think she's got real talent."

If I had ever considered bringing up Malene's cheating in this conversation, those plans were now null and void. All I wanted to do was run away from Mac as quickly as possible so that I didn't have to hear him call me the perfect subject again. It was just weird when older men did that.

"Be sure to tell her I can't wait to see what she enters next year." He winked. "Hope it's another one of you."

Gag. "I'll tell her."

I would absolutely not say one word to her like that. I did not want to have this embarrassingly icky conversation with Mac ever again. In fact, after this little chat, I'd be just fine if he avoided me for the rest of my life—and his.

"Well, I've got to get going. I've got a box of sconces in my truck just itching to be used."

"You take care."

I waved. "You too."

I slipped into my truck and drove off, wishing that the ick from the conversation would slide right off me.

It wasn't until I got home and took a long, hot shower that I felt better. How had I not realized that Mac was so lecherous? Easy. Because I hadn't been around him before.

Once the water was off and I'd wrapped myself in my favorite terry-cloth robe, I started to feel better.

I painted my toenails and dried and styled my hair.

By the time that was done, it was starting to get late. I had plans with Rufus and was glad for it. I didn't want to be in my home. I didn't want to tell him that, though, because I didn't want it to seem like I was saying that I'd only feel better at his place.

It wasn't good to manipulate my relationship in that way. If anyone is still confused by what I mean, this might explain it better: if I told Rufus that I was worried about the sprite, he might tell me to stay at his house. Well, then I'd have him all to myself, and goodness knew what would happen then. Clearly I would work the situation to my advantage, get him alone that night and, well, y'all know what would follow—Lady forcing Rufus to marry me so that she could call him her stepdaddy forever.

Anyway, it was safest for me to stay at my house, even if the idea that an invisible little devil-like creature could gain entrance to my house any time it wanted gave me the heebie-jeebies.

Anyway, Rufus picked me up a little while later for dinner. Lady insisted on coming with us as she didn't want to be home alone at night in case the sprite showed up.

"I don't trust nothing that I cain't see," she declared before getting into Rufus's SUV.

I couldn't have agreed with her more.

At dinner, I decided not to tell Rufus about the strange encounter I had with Mac. Honestly I preferred to put the entire thing completely out of my mind. Though I decided I would mention it to Malene at the very least to discourage her from using me again and also to remind her that she needed to fess up about exactly how she had won that ribbon.

I still wasn't giving up on my belief that Malene would eventually come clean. She had to. After all, wouldn't the burden of her secret hurt her in the long run? Wouldn't it make her soul decrepit? Wouldn't the guilt be crushing?

All right, so I was overexaggerating the affect that cheating would have on my grandmother. But you never knew, maybe even pigs would one day fly.

Given the state of our current world, nothing would have surprised me.

But to get my mind off Malene, at dinner, while Lady was playing doggie footsie with me under the table (and by that, I mean she had curled up on my foot, which was currently asleep), I asked Rufus about his knowledge of sprites.

"You seemed fairly perturbed about the sprite this morning." He nodded, slicing into his steak. I took a bite of my steak-topped salad, chewed and waited for him to answer. When I could tell that he wasn't going to keep talking, I continued. "You have a story about one."

He sipped his water. "I do. I'm not sure that you want to hear it."

"I want to hear anything that you have to tell me. I love talking to you."

He chuckled. "I get the feeling this story may not meet the same requirements as you love talking to me."

"Try me."

He held his fork and knife, his knuckles whitening as his hands tightened. They quickly relaxed and he began. "This happened after I met you the first time."

By that he meant when we'd originally connected and he'd attempted to steal my powers, when Rufus had been more Dark Lord than Knight in Shining Armor.

He went on. "I was living in a small magical town. Of course, I'd just arrived. The people didn't know anything about me, anything of what I was. I was only just making my way into their lives. I was figuring out my plan to dominate the town, to take the magic that I wanted and needed from them. As you know, I have been evil."

I squeezed his hand. "But aren't anymore."

He nodded but didn't reply to my comment. "A sprite was called. Only one. But it wreaked damage."

"Why? Is it just in their nature?"

"No. They're like children, angry that they've been plucked out of their homes, forced to be in a place that's foreign to them. And if you want the truth, I believe they have every right to be angry. I would be, too. But anyhow, this sprite made itself known. Whereas the one we're dealing with in Peachwood has stolen some food and broken some irreplaceable antiques of yours, the one I encountered was much more sinister."

"And it wasn't even in a group," I murmured.

"No, it wasn't. There was no confidence in numbers here. It was simply one sprite with a huge chip on its shoulder."

"What did it do?"

"What *didn't* it do would be a better question. It began playing pranks."

"What sort of pranks?" Rufus paused, which to be honest, worried me a little bit. So I pushed him. "Come on, it couldn't have been that bad."

He didn't answer that; instead he said, "The thing—the sprite—started changing the witches and wizards. A wizard would go to bed perfectly normal and would wake up with horns sprouting from its head. A woman would suddenly have green skin, covered with warts."

"Ew."

"That wasn't the worst of it. I saw one wizard with a horn sprouting from his chest. It was very painful, he said. What I witnessed were horrible, awful atrocities. And you can imagine for me to think that, they must've been bad. Because I was awful at the time, planning and plotting a way to steal magic from these people. But that plan quickly changed once I saw what was going on."

"You knew the sprite had to be stopped."

"Absolutely." He nodded hard. "There was no doubt in my mind. So I joined the wizards and witches who were unaffected. That number was quickly shrinking, by the way. Day by day, more and more people were becoming infected with whatever magic the sprite was using against us."

I did not want to wake up in the morning with horns coming out of my head or rear end. I was pretty sure that would dampen my day just a teensy bit.

"We formed a plan to catch the sprite and send it back. But of course, the first thing we had to figure out was who had called the creature in the first place. Of course, no one wanted to admit fault. It took a lot of people asking a lot of questions, and finally we found out who the culprit was."

"Who had called it?" I asked.

"A teenage girl who was angry at her parents because they wouldn't let her date the wizard of her choice. When I met him, I understood why. He was like me—wore black, had a chip on his shoulder. You know the type."

I had encountered my fair share of bad boys in my day. So yes, I knew the type.

"What happened then?" I asked.

"She showed us the spell she had used to call it. We were able to catch the sprite—which wasn't easy. We needed her help for that. That's another problem that often stems in these cases—it's hard to capture them."

"Oh," I replied, uncertain what else to say.

"But anyway, to make a long story short, we caught the creature, forced it to reverse all the spells it had cast against others, freeing them of their curses, and we sent it back to where it had come from. All in all, I think the entire encounter lasted a week, but it felt like a month. A day didn't go by that I wasn't worried I would be the next person to wind up with a horn protruding from my body. It was not a good place to be in."

"No, I wouldn't think so. I'm sorry." I added cheerfully, "But you made it out."

"Yes, and I left that town as soon as the sprite was gone. Too much bad luck after having just arrived."

He was on to something, but I sensed there was more to the reason for his leaving than that. "Do you think you also vacated because you had helped those folks and you had started to see them as actual people? Not just sheep for you to steal from?"

"Yes, I do. But I couldn't admit that to myself at the time."

"But you can now." I smiled. "You have grown so much. You are a better person now than you were then. But even then, your star was beginning to shine bright. Please don't ignore that."

A small smile tugged at his ridiculously full and luscious lips. "Thank you for believing in me."

I hadn't always; but I did then. But anyway, back to our romantic dinner.

"How about Fiji?" Rufus asked.

I nearly choked on my salad. "Fiji? For what?"

Please say for our weekend getaway. Please say that!

"For our getaway," he replied.

It took everything I had not to jump up and shout, *yes!* Somehow, I don't know how, but I managed to remain composed.

Actually, I did so by dropping my gaze to my salad and poking at the lettuce, which was starting to look a little droopy from all the dressing tossed on top of it.

"Well, um, that would be great. But don't you think it might be a tad bit extravagant?"

"No, I don't. Europe would be extravagant. This is not. It's also only for a weekend. It's not for an entire month. That would be extravagant. So. What do you say? Once we get this whole mess cleared up with the sprite?"

How could I say no to that? He was being responsible. We would deal with the sprite first. Then we would go on vacation.

I was in, baby.

"Sounds like a great plan."

He grinned. "Then I'll make it happen." He lifted his glass. "To Fiji."

I clinked my water glass against his. "To Fiji."

Lady's muffled voice came from down below. "Y'all keep it down. I'm trying to sleep, here."

Rufus and I both laughed. "Whatever you say, Lady," I told her. "Whatever you say."

Rufus dropped me off at my house a little while later. We stood on the porch, and he brushed a strand of hair from my shoulder.

"Will you be okay tonight?" he asked, the sincerity and worry evident.

"Yes, I'll be fine." I was going to Fiji. I would definitely be okay. "Don't worry about me."

"If you're sure."

"I am."

He kissed me, and we said our good nights. I led Lady inside, and we curled up in my bed. Despite being worried, I was tired and fell asleep quickly and soundly. When I awoke the next morning, it was in the same position that I'd drifted off in.

Lady, who'd been curled up at my feet, suddenly felt like she weighed a ton.

I nudged her with my leg. "Have you been eating bricks? You are so heavy."

She replied something a muffled voice. I couldn't decipher what she'd said because it sounded like her face was stuffed in the duvet.

"Come on, Lady. Get up. Seriously." I tried to move my leg, but it was stuck underneath her. "What happened to you? I can't pull my leg out from under you."

Her head popped up. Only it wasn't my dog's head. It was a woman with big brown eyes and soft chestnut hair. "I said, I didn't do nothing. I'm exactly the same as when I fell asleep."

I screamed and backed up against the headrest.

"What is it?" Lady asked.

My hands flew to my face. I sucked down several deep breaths of air. I gulped down enough to make me feel that my lungs weren't squeezing my heart anymore. (They had been. I'd just forgotten to mention it.)

"Lady," I said with a shaky voice. "You're not a dog."

"I ain't? What am I?"

"You…you're…a woman. You've been turned into a woman."

CHAPTER 15

$\mathcal{N}$ever in my entire life had I witnessed anything so insane. My dog fell asleep a dog, and she woke up a human being. What madness was this?

"Maybe I'm dreaming?" I hoped, trying to find an explanation for this craziness. "Pinch me. Never mind. You can't pinch. You're a dog."

Lady held up two fingers. "Looks like I can pinch. I'm hungry. Now I can reach the ice cream."

She hopped off my bed and strutted toward the door. Her legs were a little wobbly, but she got the hang of walking fairly quickly. I wasn't sure if that was a blessing or a curse.

A strangled cry knotted up my throat. "Clothes! You need to put clothes on."

She glanced down at her nakedness. "Do I? Oh, wow. I've got boobies. This is weird."

"There's a robe in the bathroom. Wait. I'll get it." As much as I loved spending a morning in bed—and did I ever—this was not the time to be lounging. My dog had become human. This made no sense. How could this have happened? Who could have—

Oh no. The answer hit me as soon as I asked it. The sprite. That prankster snuck into my house last night and turned my dog into a human. I bet that little creep thought it was a hysterical joke. I bet it thought that it had gotten me.

Well, it certainly had, but I wasn't going to let it know that, now was I?

I grabbed the robe and helped Lady into it. "These arms thingies are harder to maneuver than y'all make on. Maybe I'll just walk on my hands and feet."

She dropped to all fours and scurried across the floor, looking like a demon out of a horror movie.

"No, no." I took her by the arm and gently tugged her up to standing. "You need to walk like a human since you look like one."

"Okay," she said with a shrug. "If you say so. Now, where's that ice cream?"

I handed her a spoon and grabbed a bowl, but Lady yanked the lid off the tub of Blue Bell, stuck her spoon in, and brought a sliver to her mouth.

Okay, no bowl. She took the half-gallon tub to the table and glanced at a chair. My dog looked like a human who didn't want to drop her bone to grab a drink of water for fear someone would run off with her prize, but she desperately, and I mean desperately, wanted that drink.

"Here. Let me help you." I pulled the chair out, but she still stared at it. "Like this. You bend your knees and then sit."

Lady bent one knee, then the other, and scuttled to the chair like a beach crab.

Hey. Whatever worked.

She sat with an exhale, dropped the ice cream in front of her and exclaimed, "How you walk with legs is beyond me. I want my furry four legs back. It's a lot easier—to sit, anyway."

The ice cream hadn't thawed, but that wasn't stopping her from jamming the spoon into the frosty crust and taking a bite. I didn't have the heart to explain to Lady about lactose intolerance. It would just be best if she found that out for herself.

"So…you're human. You're a woman," I prodded.

Don't ask me why I was prodding. I should've been on the horn making phone calls, but I wanted to wrap my head around this situation for myself first. Then I would call Rufus and Malene, and perhaps a psychiatrist to make sure that I hadn't gone mental.

Lady lifted her bronzed arms. "Looks like it. I look about as human as they come."

Her gaze darted to the window. Suddenly she was up and scratching at the pane, barking so loudly I had to cover my ears. "A-whooo! A-whooo! Get out of my yard. I will chomp your bones up!"

Oh my. I darted over and put my hands on her arms. It was only then that I spotted a lone squirrel dashing across the top of the wooden fence.

Boy, was I in trouble or what?

"Okay, Lady." I directed her back to the seat and gave her a little push to help her sit better. "The first rule about being human is that you can't act like a dog."

Her foot came up toward her neck, and she said, agitated, "I have an itch. Argh. I cain't reach it."

I took her hand and ran the fingers over her throat. "That's how human's scratch. We use our hands. Not our feet."

"Feet are just as good," she mumbled.

There was no way in all the world that I would be able to take her out in public. She'd be committed to a loony bin within ten minutes of romping around with the general population.

"So Lady, did you feel anything funny last night?"

She had resumed her focus on the ice cream and paused to think of my question. "When you say funny, how do you mean?"

"Like any strange tingles?" I guessed that was what it would feel like to become human. "Any weirdness?"

She pulled the spoon from her lips, leaving a streak of chocolate along one side of her mouth. Don't worry, the other side was already streaked. She ate like a toddler.

"Nope. I didn't feel no weirdness. I just fell right to sleep. But I did notice something."

"What was it?" This could have been a clue! It could be the sign that I needed that would help me figure out how to change her back. "What did you sense?"

"Well, my legs were hanging off the bed. That was strange. That had never happened before."

My hopes crashed to the ground. "Was that all you noticed?"

"Yep. Then of course, you told me that I was an actual lady, not meaning my name."

"Okay, well. Just stay here for a minute."

She paused, spoon midway to her mouth. "Why? Where you going?"

"I'm going to call Rufus. See if he can come over and figure something out."

She stared down at the silky robe. "I ain't even decent. You cain't call him."

"I'll let you borrow some of my clothes. You can change before he gets here."

"I hate to point this out to you, but I'm smaller than you are."

She was tall, resembling the length of her dachshund body. But Lady was also thin, like model thin, as if she only ate grapes and drank a glass of wine a day, thin.

I read that in the food journal of someone famous and thin. All they ate one day was a few grapes and a couple glasses of wine. Not sure how they managed not to kill someone that day from being overly hangry.

If I started a diet like that, I would commit murder by sundown. No doubt about it.

But back to Lady's question about clothes. "I'll get a belt and tighten any pants at the waist."

She blinked at me slowly. Oh no. My dog in human form was a diva. "I don't think it'll work."

"It will. You just need a little faith."

"Clem, I got faith up to my furry ears, but what you're talking about is a miracle."

I pursed my lips together, doing my best to ignore the fact that my dog had just not so politely called me fat. "I think that I've been alive long enough to be able to look at someone and guess their size."

"I would think so, but you're wrong."

Now I had to rise to the test. "I'll prove it. Stay here."

I strode into my kitchen, cheeks hot at the fact that my dog, my *dog*, had said that I was chunkier than her. I charged into my closet and quickly located the section of jeans that were too small but that I still kept.

Okay, I didn't think it was any big secret that women held on to clothing that they hoped they would fit into someday. Some of those jeans had been purchased *before* I started eating chocolate for breakfast.

Yes, eating chocolate had put a couple of extra pounds on me. I didn't regret it. I thought that I looked a little curvier, a little more filled out.

Also, some of the pants were purchased because I loved them. Like, couldn't live without them kind of love. I tried them on and knew that I needed to drop maybe two or three pounds—just enough that I could breathe when I wore them. All right, so I didn't lose the weight, but I still kept hold of the pants. Because, you know, one day.

Apparently one day had arrived. But it wasn't my day. It was my dog's. How insane did that sound? To admit that I couldn't fit into my jeans, but my dog, who was now human, could?

It was as if the heavens were the earth and the earth was the heavens. You know, because everything had become tilted, off-kilter, wonky.

I grabbed a couple of pairs of pants and a top or two that were smalls (also from my pre-chocolate days). One of them was an adorable red blouse with a sweetheart neckline. I really liked it. Perhaps I should have given up chocolate just to fit into it again.

It seemed like a hard sacrifice. One that I wasn't sure that I was willing to make.

I took them into the kitchen and found Lady had eaten nearly all the ice cream. Fudge-colored streaks lined her cheeks and mouth.

"What did you do? Stick your head in the container?" I asked.

"How else was I supposed to get to the good stuff?"

"The spoon. Humans use spoons."

She held it like a knife that she was about to jab into someone's back. "This the right way?"

"No. That is absolutely not the correct method unless you plan to commit murder."

"What? I ain't no murderer. Unless we're talking about squirrels."

I rolled my eyes. "Here are some clothes. Let's see what fits."

It didn't take long for me to find a pair of jeans, T-shirt, and panties that fit Lady. I was also able to get her into one of my bras as well. I considered that the luckiest part of my morning. If we hadn't been the same size cup, that could've been bad. Like, swing lo, sweet chariot, bad.

When Lady was fully dressed, I took a step back and drew a breath. My dog was a knockout.

This was a problem, mainly because she wasn't human. Maybe she wouldn't need to go outside and see the world through her human eyes.

Just then, Lady lifted her armpit and sniffed. "Okay, it's not me that smells bad." She marched over, picked up my arm and dug her nose into my armpit. "It's you. You need a shower, Clem. You smell like you're stressed out."

Scratch my earlier statement about maybe Lady not needing to go outside. Unless we were under threat of nuclear attack and the only way to survive was to join up with a band of Peachwood witches, there was no way in Hades that Lady would ever, and I mean ever, interact with other humans.

My phone rang, and Malene's name lit up the screen. Oh, good. She was calling me first. What a doozie this bit of information would be.

"Hey, Malene, there's something—"

My grandmother's voice was overflowing with angst. "Clem, you've got to come here now."

"Where? Your house?"

"No downtown. Something's happened."

"Can't you tell me what?"

"No time. Get down here, now. The fate of Peachwood depends on it."

CHAPTER 16

I had a good grip on Lady. If truth be known, it was a death grip. An actual death grip, or at least as close as I could get without strangling her.

When we got into my truck, I called Rufus. "I'm heading downtown. Malene called. Said something happened."

"Everything okay?" he asked as if sensing that an actual tragedy had occurred in my life.

I was looking for parking and didn't want to go into it, so I simply replied, "I'll tell you when I see you. Meet me downtown."

"I'll be there soon."

We hung up, and Lady exclaimed (with her face hanging out the window), "My stepdaddy's finally going to see me as a person. This is wonderful."

I grabbed a handful of her shirt and pulled her back in. "News flash —only dogs hang their heads from windows."

She stared at me blankly. "And?"

"And you can't forget that you are a dog trapped in a human's body. You don't do things like put your head out. Right? That's not something that a beautiful woman would do."

She scowled. "I don't like this whole being-human thing. Too many rules."

"I'm sorry about that, but it's just the way it goes."

"You still didn't have to yell at me over the whole bathroom thing. How was I supposed to remember that I needed to use a toilet?"

And yes, the most harrowing part of my morning occurred when Lady squatted in the middle of my floor—fully clothed. It took me all of three seconds to figure out what was going on. I dragged her into the bathroom and quickly instructed her on what to do.

When she exited a minute later, I had to remind her to button her jeans.

This was going to be a long day.

We reached downtown, and I found a spot on a side street to park. After switching off the ignition, I turned to Lady. "No matter what you see, no matter what you smell, no matter what you hear, you stay right beside me. You do not run off. You do not sniff people's crotches now that you can reach them. You do not sniff people's legs or shoes or their faces. Do you understand?"

She gave me a frosty glance. "I get it."

Time to reinforce the idea. "Because if you act weird, people will wonder about you, and then we'll have a whole other problem on our hands."

"I ain't a problem." She crossed her arms. "I am a dog, and dogs are man's and women's best friend."

"Yes, you are." I patted her head to soothe her. "But you are a dog in human form. That makes things different. So." I unsnapped my safety belt. "Are you ready?"

"As ready as I'm gonna be."

"Let's go."

It took everything in me not to have brought a body leash for Lady. Not that I owned one. Even if I had, it would've been too small. It would've been dachshund-sized instead of big enough to fit a Saint Bernard. You see how this would've been a problem.

But anyhow, after we parked, I walked as close to Lady as possible, doing my best to make sure that a chittering squirrel didn't grab her attention.

When she didn't run off or sniff every fire hydrant we walked by (and trust me, I could tell that she was tempted), I eased up a little and gave her some space.

Perhaps Lady could do this. Maybe she would be a good human—at least for a few hours until we figured out how to turn her back into a dog.

"I don't know how you can stand shoes." She stopped to twist and turn her ankles. "These are about the worst invention ever. Lawd, I cain't wait to get back to my old self."

That made two of us.

"Well, the sooner we run into Rufus, the quicker he'll be able to find magic that will fix you."

"Oh, but then I won't get to pretend that I'm your cousin from far away."

I smirked. "Why would you want to do that?"

"So that I can find out how he feels about you. Get him to tell me when he's going to propose, when he'll officially become my stepdaddy."

I choked on a bit of saliva. A coughing fit took hold, and it was a couple minutes before my lungs calmed down and we were able to walk again.

"Please don't call him that to his face," I croaked. "I don't think I could handle it."

"You want the truth? You cain't handle the truth!" She laughed. "Just kidding. I saw that in a movie once. It starred Tom Cruise. You know, 'cause I turn the TV on when you're gone."

"Some things you should just really keep from me."

"If it makes you feel better, I was trying to find the nature channel."

"That actually doesn't."

She shrugged as if that was neither here nor there. "Well, where are we going? What are we here for?"

"I don't know, but I have a feeling we'll recognize it when we see it."

We rounded a corner, heading straight for the center of downtown. I dug in my heels and sucked air.

Well, I'd been right about one thing. When I saw it, I knew it.

The spot downtown where a fountain sat and where the food trucks lined up and where folks sat at tables and on benches was sheer havoc.

Tables and chairs were roped together. The fountain that lit up at nighttime, the one that water rippled from, now had pee-colored water flowing over it. There weren't any food trucks parked along the street.

Thank goodness for that. I would've hated to see what the sprite would have done to them. From the looks of it, there was no telling.

Malene called from the middle of the melee. "Clem, I'm so glad you're here. Hurry! Come and see!"

She stood with Urleen and Norma Ray at the fountain. The three of them stared into the water as if captivated by the amount of pee that was before them.

As Lady and I got closer, I was holding my nose. But after a few seconds I realized that I wasn't an Olympic scuba diver or anything. My lungs hurt, and I was dying for a breath. I inhaled and exhaled with relief.

The water did not smell like urine. It only looked like it. That was a plus.

"What are y'all looking at?" I asked.

"At the octopus in the water," Norma Ray said. "Malene said that we should just magic it away, but Urleen insists that if we get rid of it, something worse will happen."

I blinked. "Worse than pee-colored water and tables that are all messed up?"

"Mm hmm," admitted Urleen. "Worse than that." She opened her handbag and started rummaging through it as she spoke. "Why else would the sprite have left the octopus here? It's some sort of safeguard. Get rid of it, and something else happens. Keep it and everything will be fine."

"We can't keep an octopus in the fountain," Malene griped. "Someone will take it out eventually." Her gaze landed on Lady. "Clem, who's your friend? And is she in the know?" my grandmother asked, hand cupped to her mouth as if sharing a secret.

"So it appears pranking downtown isn't the only thing that the sprite did last night." I gestured to Lady. "Allow me to present Lady, my dachshund in human form."

Their mouths dropped in unison. They stared at Lady for a moment. I expected them to be horrified. I expected them to grimace and shake their heads at the ridiculousness of it all.

I did not expect them to fawn over her.

"Why, look at that pretty hair," Norma Ray said.

"And she's got such big eyes," Urleen quipped.

"And what a figure." Malene's gaze washed up and down her. "Clem, you could take some notes from her. Maybe quit the chocolate for a bit."

What was it with the chocolate? First I'd been beating myself up about it, and now here was Malene telling me that I could stand to lose a few pounds off the old hips.

I hated it when my conscious and others were right.

"Hey, y'all." Lady gave a little finger wave. Then, very proudly, she added, "Clem had to go into the dark corner of her closet to find clothes that would fit me."

My jaw dropped. "How do you know?"

She shot me a smug smile. "Because I may be human, but I can still hear as good as a dog." She sniffed. "I can smell good, too, and that there octopus smells fishy."

Malene patted her hand. "I rather like you as a human."

"You will until she squats on your living room floor to take a dump," I murmured.

Malene's eyes narrowed. "Nonsense. You're just jealous. Now. It appears the sprite has been busy. Lady, we will eventually have to deal with you, because you shouldn't be human. But first, we have to deal with the fountain."

"I see that I'm just in time."

Rufus strode up behind us. I have to say that he looked dashing in his leather pants, dark shirt and jacket. How did he manage to look so cool and edgy in a small town? And the weirdest part was that it actually worked for him. Like, he could make any outfit seem normal.

Okay, maybe he couldn't make Bermuda shorts look normal. There was no one who could do that except maybe Jimmy Buffet. But Jimmy had been at his whole look a long time. Jimmy was more of a lifestyle kind of person than a look. That was why the whole Margaritaville thing worked out for him.

Anyway, off the tangent and back to reality. Rufus took one look into the fountain and proclaimed, "It's a trap."

Urleen shot everyone a triumphant look. "Exactly as I said."

"I was going to say it," Malene insisted. "You just had to give me more time."

"No, you weren't," Norma Ray argued. "You weren't going to say that. In fact, you wanted to get rid of the octopus as soon as you could. I think you were waiting for our backs to be turned so that you could fish it out and stomp on it."

Malene gasped. "I would never have done such a callous, violent thing. I would have simply let it suffocate on the ground."

Urleen and Norma Ray exchanged a knowing look. "Not much difference," Norma Ray said after a moment.

"I beg your pardon, but there is."

While the women argued, I got Rufus's attention. "This is Lady."

His eyes flared. "I'm sorry?"

"So, the sprite didn't set off any of the booby traps last night. Instead it changed Lady from a dog into this."

"Human," Rufus croaked. "Oh dear. This is worse than I thought."

"Really? How could it be worse than you thought?"

"It's just more magical than I previously believed. But this sprite, it has a lot of power. Perhaps the creature angry at you for some reason."

Angry at me? How could the sprite be angry at me? I was the one who should have been ticked at it. After all, it had destroyed that antique glass paperweight and now it had turned my dog into a person. Lady as a dog was bad enough. Now I had to deal with the fact that she was beautiful *and* had no filter on her mouth. Before, I could just make her stay home if she got on my nerves. But now…what was I supposed to do with her? She could open doors, walk right out of my house.

Lady could even try to drive my truck if she wanted to.

Okay, before I started hyperventilating, I needed to inhale and exhale, not get ahead of myself.

There. That was better.

What was it that had bothered me again?

Oh, right. Lady being out in the world alone, all by herself, being charmed by men and then stopping to sniff every fire hydrant she walked past.

Rufus interrupted my thoughts with, "We've got to take one problem at a time. First, the fountain, as it's our most central problem at the moment."

"Right, the octopus," I replied. "Exactly why do you think it's a trap?"

He gestured to the fountain. "Why else would it be here?"

"What I said," Urleen pointed out. "Precisely."

Rufus explained farther. "The octopus is meant to look like it doesn't matter if we get rid of it, but there's no other reason for it to be in the fountain. Unless the sprite simply wanted to go for shock value, but I don't think that's what's at play here. It was placed in the fountain for us to take out. And once we do that, something worse will happen."

I watched as the creature curled its tentacles together and shot across the fountain until it reached the other end of the stone structure. Then it rotated and repeated the move, jetting to the opposite end, back to us.

"What should we do?" Norma Ray asked.

"We should change everything back very carefully," Rufus replied. "Which is why I brought a restore orb with me."

"Oh, that was smart." Norma Ray nodded enthusiastically. "You are such a forward thinker."

Somebody had to be. "But will it work, or will it trigger the next thing the sprite wanted to happen?"

"I think it will work. The magic attached to this orb returns things to the way that they were. It's not meant to interfere, just reverse."

Everyone was quiet for a moment. We were all thinking the same thing. The spell could work, or it could go terribly wrong. Either way, we didn't have much choice.

"Let's do it," I said.

"Very well."

Rufus released the magic within the orb. A quick flash of light penetrated the area, and in a blink, it was gone. The water leaking from the fountain had returned to its natural color. The tables and chairs were right. Lady was still human.

Drat. I had hoped maybe that would change.

"Well," Rufus said with a victorious smile, "looks like we won this round."

A rumble erupted from the fountain. All of us shifted back, staring at the structure. The very top of the concrete pedestal exploded into the sky, and a huge, story-tall tentacle reached out into the air.

"Well," Rufus said grimly. "So much for winning this round. Looks like it's time to fight a giant octopus."

$\mathcal{I}$ stared, slack-jawed, as the octopus's tentacle jutted into the air and crashed down on a portion of the fountain, shattering it and spraying stone, or whatever they make fountains out of, everywhere.

"I think we've done it now," Malene shouted. "Run!"

People, regular people, the sort that shouldn't see things like this, screamed in the background. It suddenly felt like I'd been swept away from Peachwood and deposited smack-dab in the middle of a superhero movie. Preferably ones starring Henry Cavill.

But anyway, while people screamed and I stared at the fountain, watching as the octopus rose like a phoenix from the ashes to destroy us all, Rufus jumped into action.

He shoved a bag in my hands. "Here. Take these."

"What are they?"

"Orbs. Use them against the creature. We've got to stop it!"

Now that, I didn't have to be told. Yes, we had to stop the creature. That had become abundantly clear when the creature's head jutted out of the fountain—inky black eyes stared menacingly around and a giant beak opened and the creature screeched.

I felt like I'd witnessed this scene before. In my dreams, perhaps? An episode of Scooby-Doo? I didn't know and it didn't matter. What *did* matter was that we stopped the octopus before it did any more damage.

Just then, one of its tentacles swept across the ground and sent a wrought-iron table crashing into a storefront.

"We're going to have a hard time explaining this," Malene shrieked.

"Ah, the tentacles are after me," Norma Ray shouted.

Sure enough, the octopus curled its arm around Norma Ray and lifted her in the air.

"I'm too old for this," she shouted. "Somebody save me! But make sure he's handsome and has a full head of hair."

"At your age, you'll be lucky if he's able to pull his pants up by himself," Urleen called up to her.

Rufus jumped into action, throwing orbs at the other, less busy tentacles. The octopus flinched and apparently Rufus's tactic worked, because it opened its arm and released Norma Ray.

Rufus threw another orb onto the ground. Out of its center sprang a landing cushion, one that Norma Ray fell not so softly onto.

"That's enough adventure to last me the rest of my life," she wailed.

Meanwhile Lady had taken off and was attacking the octopus's base, barking and biting at it.

Ugh. I just…couldn't go there. I didn't have the energy to stop her and call her back. People would see what they were going to see no matter what.

So I started tossing orbs at the creature. "What sort of magic did you give me?" I asked Rufus.

"I have no idea. It's sort of a mixed bag. All we need to do is destroy it."

I gaped at him. "Then we'll be stuck with a huge dead octopus."

He tossed an orb that exploded to the right of the creature. It shrieked in anger, and I swear that fury filled its big black eyes.

Rufus ducked as a tentacle lashed out at him. "What would you rather me do, wish it away somewhere, to a place where it could do more damage?"

"What about the bottom of the ocean?" I moved quickly to avoid being struck by another groping arm. "That would be perfect for it. It could live out the rest of its life there, swimming with other strange ocean creatures."

"What about when it attacks a submarine?" He tossed an orb and missed. "How will you live with the guilt when an entire vessel full of seamen and women perish?"

"You've really thought this through." His ability to think on the fly was impressive. But I was not to be deterred. "What about outer space?"

He scoffed. "So it can suffocate to death? You really are not very kind."

I hurled an orb at the creature, hitting it squarely at the base of its, um, body. I think that was what it was called. You know, where the roundish area met the long feet. Was that a body? Or just an oversize head? Anyway, the orb exploded, causing the octopus to shrink back.

But only for a second.

Then it started to move.

Like, walk, with big curling tentacles that unfurled. The suckers latched onto the ground, and the creature used that hold to slowly tug itself forward.

"Oh no, it's trying to escape! What do we do?"

"We stop it," Rufus said, jaw firmly set, eyes narrowed, looking extraordinarily handsome even though the world was collapsing all around us. "Throw everything you've got at it."

Rufus rushed ahead, trying to cut off the octopus before it was able to leave the perimeter.

Malene shouted, "Come on, girls! Grab a weapon and let's go!"

"A weapon?" The innocence in Norma Ray's voice sometimes grated on me. "What sort?"

Malene shoved a two-by-four that had broken off a bench when the octopus smashed it into her hands. "Take this. We've got to help Rufus."

Urleen dug into her purse and pulled out a cattle prod. I blinked to make sure that I was actually seeing what I thought. Yes, that was a cattle prod.

"I'm ready," she yelled.

Why in the world did Urleen have a cattle prod in her purse? Well, if there was one thing that I could say, it was that Urleen always came prepared.

Lady, meanwhile, was still barking and snarling at the octopus. I raced over, grabbed her by the scruff of her collar and yanked her back.

"Come on! You can't be that close to it. We're going to hit it with everything we've got." At least, I thought that was the plan. Even if it wasn't, Lady couldn't keep attacking it like that. Eventually the octopus would smash her or something.

"Let me at it," she snarled.

"No! Come with me."

I dragged her from the creature and joined up with everyone else. Since we'd given the huge blob a wider berth, it started moving faster.

Also, an entire crowd of people had gathered, ringing the perimeter of the square. Like, didn't they know this was a dangerous situation? If a volcano was set to erupt, would those same folks rush to watch it blow its top?

The short and sad answer was probably yes, they would.

We half ringed the creature, and that was when Rufus yelled, "Attack!"

Normally I would have told the old ladies to stay home. Normally I would not have been faced with fighting an oversize octopus. Normally I would have been eating lunch right about now.

But nothing about this was normal.

We hit the creature hard, attacking it with everything that we had. Urleen shoved the cattle prod into it, but it didn't seem to affect the octopus at all. Malene and Norma Ray attacked with their wood, but once again, their assault had no effect on the larger-than-life ghostbusters-style huge fish, or octopod, or whatever category octopuses fit into.

Was *octopuses* even a word? Or was the correct term *octopi*?

I didn't know, and I didn't care to ever look it up. This was about as close and personal as I was ever going to get to a creature like this for the rest of my life.

Or so I prayed.

Anyway, Rufus hit the creature with orb after orb, as did I. The orbs slowed it but did not stop it. What would?

Magic buzzed in the air, making my head swim. Y'all, it was like I was singing in church and suddenly the Holy Ghost had taken over my body. I was acting without thinking, acting and moving without any brain hiccups telling me to stop.

The next thing I knew, a magical spear was in my hand, waiting to be released. It was big, y'all, as thick as three broom handles. And heavy.

Really heavy. It was so heavy that part of my brain said, *You're never going to be able to throw that,* and then the other half replied back, *Whether you believe that you can or you can't, you're right.*

Yeah, I know. I was getting really deep.

Anyway, a spark of belief ignited in my chest. Next thing I knew, the spear was hurtling toward the octopus. Usually I could only throw a baseball about twenty or thirty feet, but this projectile was fueled by rockets or something.

It soared across the sky and hit the octopus right between the eyes.

The whole world stopped. Everything seemed to slow down. The impact of the spear made me shudder. The octopus reared back, surprised by the hit. Then it wiggled and shivered as if in laughter.

But the octopus wasn't laughing. Instead the jiggling intensified, and Rufus said, "It's gonna blow! Everyone take cover!"

Well you've never seen old ladies move so fast. Urleen, Norma Ray and Malene darted behind an overturned table. I grabbed Lady, who I sensed still wanted to be in the middle of the melee, and pulled her behind Rufus, who tossed an orb to the ground. Where it landed, a translucent shield erupted from the ground, guarding us.

I watched in horror as the octopus, still not advancing, still not retreating, simply shuddered like a bowl of Jell-O.

I had felt so much fear for it, and that fear wasn't gone. My fists were up, ready to return to fighting any second. But what had come over me? How had that spear been formed? Had I unconsciously summoned it? Had I *consciously* summoned it and I just hadn't realized it because I'd been so busy with everything else?

I didn't know, and as much as I wanted answers in that exact moment, I realized that I wasn't going to get them.

"Are you sure that thang's gonna blow?" Lady asked Rufus.

He nodded. "It's about to."

The shuddering intensified, and a high-pitched whining noise spewed from the octopus.

Rufus murmured. "And three, two, o—"

It exploded into a million pieces. Big hunks of gooey black stuff rained down in the air, landing all around us. I heard screams behind me, probably from eyewitnesses who had us confused with the family from the *Incredibles* movies.

There was black goop everywhere. It looked like a tar truck had exploded. Goodness, that was going to be a lot of clean up.

I really, really didn't like that sprite.

My heart knocked against my ribs, and it took a few seconds before I glanced up at Rufus and said, "I'm glad that's over."

He nodded. "Me too. You saved us with the spear."

Oh, uh. Yeah. It just appeared out of nowhere."

And then a sound that made my skin tingle filled the air—laughter. But not just any laughter, the sprite's laughter echoed in the area.

All of us heard it. Malene, Urleen and Norma Ray all had worried looks on their faces. Rufus pulled me a little tighter to him. Lady's eyes narrowed. She opened her mouth to bark, and I shook my head, "Don't," I said curtly.

As quickly as the laughter had struck, it vanished, leaving us with a goopy mess to clean up. "Well," I said after I'd come out from behind the shield, "who's ready to grab a broom and clean up?"

Just then, a trio of boys on bikes zipped into the area. They were the same ones that I'd seen before with packs slung over their shoulders. One of them was slightly opened and inside were orbs.

Orbs.

That was what I'd seen them carrying the other day, but I'd convinced myself that the boys didn't have orbs, that they weren't dabbling in magic.

Now there was no denying the truth.

The first boy looked at us and said, "It's all our faults. We're sorry."

Rufus sighed. With his jaw set firm he said, "Help clean up this mess, and then tell us everything you've done."

CHAPTER 18

The police showed up a few minutes later. That was fun. Tuney Sluggs moseyed on up in his cowboy boots and cowboy hat, taking a look at that bit of goopy mess that Rufus's magic hadn't gotten to yet.

The chief of police rubbed his cheek and spat out a line of brown saliva. Ugh. I hated it when men chewed tobacco and then spit out the gunky stuff in front of me. It was so disgusting.

"Well, what do we have here?" Sluggs asked.

A giant octopus that almost ate us, I nearly answered.

But Rufus didn't miss a beat. "A weather balloon came down and caused some havoc. But we got rid of it very quickly."

"Weather balloon, huh?" Sluggs was not convinced. "Do they even have those things anymore?"

"Oh yes," Norma Ray answered. "Don't you remember when that one family claimed that their son was caught in one and they called emergency services? The police chased the weather balloon for miles until the boy was found safely at the family's house." She gave Sluggs a triumphant look. "The boy told on them, though. Said that the family pulled the publicity stunt because they were about to get their own television show—some B cable network, I think. But anyway, yes, weather balloons still exist."

Tuney Sluggs's eyes were round as saucers. I didn't think he expected Norma Ray to have such a good answer for him. He cleared his throat. "Some folks said something about a monster."

"A monster?" Rufus scoffed. "I highly doubt there's been a monster. If there was a monster, don't you think all of us would've seen it? No. There wasn't anything like that. Just a weather balloon."

Okay, so I got *why* Rufus wasn't telling Sluggs everything. It was hard to know how the chief would react. Would he throw us in jail because we were magical and the octopus was created by magic? He was a little hard to predict at times, I would say that. The chief either overreacted or he completely underreacted. Either way was not good until we knew exactly what was going on. Besides, since we were dealing with magic, we were the best people to handle the situation instead of cops. They weren't exactly trained in how to defend against the dark arts, now where they?

In response to Rufus dismissing Sluggs's claims that there had been a monster anywhere near the area, Sluggs gave the black goop a good once-over with his beady little eyes. "Doesn't quite look like a weather balloon."

"They make them out of new stuff now," Urleen assured him. "They're not all shiny silvery stuff."

"I hear they may rethink the design," Malene added. "This new substance is awfully heavy. I believe that's why it fell from the sky. And look"—she pointed to an overturned table that we hadn't righted yet—"they're so heavy that when they land, they cause real destruction."

We all grinned at Sluggs, in unison, as if we were on a game show and hamming it up for the camera. His gaze darted around a bit uneasily, but after a long moment he said in resignation, "Fine. Just y'all get it cleaned up. But if I hear of any more rumors of monsters, I'll be visiting y'all's houses to find out what's going on."

"Sounds fair," Malene replied, smoothing a hand over her hair. "Toodle-oo."

Once Sluggs was gone, I could breathe again. We finished cleaning up the mess, including fixing the smashed window. After that, people started returning to the area. Feeling that we were being overrun, Rufus took the first boy by his collar and growled, "The three of you, follow me."

Well, all of us followed him around the corner to a parking lot that had a few parked cars but was deserted of people.

Good. A place where we could chat.

I surveyed the three boys, who now pushed their bikes. They reminded me of kids from a movie—*The Goonies,* maybe. Kids who banded together to go on an adventure or to fight evil. Looking at them was like reliving my childhood. Except I never summoned anything when I was young. I never carried orbs, and I had never been directly involved in a giant octopus attempting to destroy a small town.

Okay, so actually, I had absolutely nothing in common with those boys. There wasn't even one girl between them. Which I supposed was a good thing because Rufus was always running around with me and Malene and her gang. There was a high estrogen to testosterone ratio in that matchup. Of course, Malene was probably so old that her body didn't even know what estrogen was anymore.

Was that mean to say?

My body would eventually be there, too. It wasn't like I wasn't saying anything that wasn't true.

Anyhow, Rufus directed his attention to the boy who had spoken to begin with. "Who are you?"

"I'm Mikey," said the fair-haired blond. "This is Cory."

Cory, a bigger boy with short spiral curls and dark skin, raised his hand. "Hey." His shining white teeth were perfect. I bet he had a nice smile.

"And this"—Mikey pointed to the last boy, a pudgy kid with glasses —"is Tank."

He didn't look like a Tank. He looked more like something a tank would roll over onto.

The boys were maybe close to ten. They weren't teenagers yet, and I could tell they were the type to spend their Saturdays on their bikes instead of playing video games. Wait. Perhaps I was giving them too much credit. Maybe they were the type to spend Saturday playing games until their moms kicked them out of the house and told them they needed to go outside and play.

That sounded more like what went on with that generation.

But anyway, back to Mikey. And Rufus, who looked ticked. "Tell me what you meant when you said this was all your fault. What is?"

The boys hung their heads. Cory peered up. "This mess. That creature. The pantries going missing. It's all our faults."

Tank opened a backpack and pulled out an ivory-colored orb. He dropped it into Rufus's open palm. "We found these."

"And a cave," Mikey added. "Down in the bluffs."

"What bluffs?" Rufus asked.

"The ones on the edge of an old neighborhood," Malene said sourly. "There are bluffs down there. Lots of kids play in them. But I've never heard of orbs being found in one."

"They were hidden, way back," Cory explained eagerly. "There was a rock covering a hole. We pushed it back and went inside."

"Went inside a cave?" I asked, shocked. "Don't you boys know that's dangerous? The cave could've collapsed. There are sinkholes out there, where you're talking about—that neighborhood."

There were indeed some sinkholes. But that had never stopped folks from living out there. Every time one of those homes went on the market, someone quickly gobbled it up. No new buildings were being put in that area, so the real estate prices were high, very high. Too rich for my blood, as folks tended to say.

Rufus backed up my worry regarding safety. "Clementine is right. You should have been more careful. But...since you went inside anyway, tell us what you found."

The boys exchanged a look. Tank spoke. "We'd heard that people were getting magic back."

"Yeah, and when we saw those floating lights, we figured they were magic," Cory added.

"Some of us said we needed to be careful," Mikey said sharply. "I told y'all."

"We thought we were being careful," Tank said. "We found a book."

Oh no. This was where things got bad.

Cory spoke. "We read the book, and the magic seemed easy."

"I didn't want to," Mikey said.

But you know, peer pressure, was what he didn't add on to the end of that statement.

Rufus pressed his fingers to his eyes. "Let me guess, you found a spell for a friend or a trickster to come."

"A playmate," Cory admitted. "That was what the book said it was. So…"

"You called it," Norma Ray finished for him. "You called what you thought would be a fun little kid to play with, and wound up with a sprite."

"One that's powerful enough to summon giant octopuses," Urleen said sadly.

Was it summoned or created? Since now was not the time to dispute her claim, I kept my mouth shut.

But just between us, I thought the creature was created.

"Do you have the book?" Rufus asked.

"No, we left it at the cave," Cory explained. "At first we thought the spell hadn't worked. Nothing happened after we said it. The balls of light kept floating around, and it wasn't like in the movies when a wind whips through the room and blows out the candles."

"Did you have candles?" Norma Ray asked.

Because *that* was important.

"No," Tank said. "No candles."

"Well, that's why none of them were blown out," Norma Ray added with a self-satisfied nod of the head. "Simple solution."

"Can we get back to the story?" Lady said impatiently. "I'm dying to know what happened next."

The boys all turned to the new voice. When their gazes landed on Lady, their eyes opened just a little bit bigger. Oh, Lawd. I had to get that dog turned back into a dog ASAP. If the reaction of children was any gauge as to Lady's sex appeal, we would be in trouble when grown men laid eyes on her.

"Well," Mikey said slowly, "nothing happened at first. Everything was quiet."

"Yeah," Cory said. "We thought that the spell was just a bunch of bull crap."

"But you took orbs with you," Rufus remarked. "Magical orbs—ones that you can see because each of you must have a touch of magic running through your veins."

"Yes!" Tank pumped his fist. "I knew that I was meant to be a wizard. Now I can go live on top of a mountain and control lightning and thunder."

"Hold on a second there, Gandalf," Rufus said. "It's a big leap from having a little bit of magic to being able to work complicated spells."

Mikey rolled his eyes. "Told you."

Tank frowned.

"So when did you work the spell?" Rufus asked.

"A few days ago," Mikey said. "Saturday."

Rufus rubbed his chin. "That was after the art show, when the jewelry went missing."

That was food for thought. I'd been so sure that the sprite had taken the jewelry. But if he hadn't done it, then who had?

But the sprite had stolen the pantry food from the church. I'd found his tie there. He'd also stolen the food from my kitchen. So there was no doubt about his guilt in that.

"Okay, so we know the sprite's been loose several days, and worse, it seems like its powers are growing," Rufus said to me.

I replied, "But now we have a way to perhaps stop it."

And we did. The book that the boys had found, if it had been what unleashed the sprite, then we could reverse the spell to send it back, exactly as Rufus had said that we could. In fact, we could head to the bluff right now, and then once we got there, we could do the magic and by suppertime everything would be back to normal.

This was great. This was perfect. We could do this.

"There's only one problem," Rufus said.

My heart sank. How could there be a problem? We had our solution lined up in front of us. What obstacle could be in our way now?

"What's that?" I asked, my voice sinking as much as my heart.

Rufus glanced at Lady. "I don't know how to turn her back into a dog. What she's under, that's more than a glamour. I'm not sure that I could reverse engineer a spell like that."

"That's not the only bad news," Tank said.

Now what? "What's that?"

He shivered. "To get to the cave, you've got to get by a really big, really mean dog."

CHAPTER 19

There was indeed a big, scary dog in the one yard that led to the one path that a person could take to get down to the bluff.

Malene, Urleen and Norma Ray had gone home to get on the phones and call everyone they knew and tell them that there was a sprite loose in Peachwood and that they needed to be on alert. The sprite could get into any home it wanted to, and it could now conjure up gigantic octopuses.

Still thought that could be *octopi*.

But anyway, I also took Lady home. We didn't need her at the moment, and she was hungry anyway (go figure). So I showed her how to make lunch and left her to it. The only stipulation was that she was not allowed to answer the front door or the house phone. I didn't want anyone to start asking questions about who she was.

So that left Rufus and me with the Hardy boys. Just kidding. I'm wasn't even sure any of them had Hardy as a last name.

After we'd made formal introductions, we set off to the house that the boys told us guarded the path down to the bluff.

The yard was open. The dog was locked inside one of those invisible fences. It wasn't a small dog, either. No, this was a Rottweiler. Big and black, with bulging muscles on its legs, the dog looked fierce—like it-would-rip-your-face-off kind of fierce.

It shook its head, and drool slung from its jowls. As if looking mean wasn't bad enough, it was also a very slimy dog.

Gross.

The five of us stood behind a large hedgerow, just out of the dog's sight.

"How do you normally get around it?" Rufus asked.

"One of us pretends to be bait while Tank gets by, and then we run outside of the fence, wait for it to lose interest in us and then we sneak around it," Mikey explained.

"We don't have time for that." Rufus shook his head. "I'll work a sleeping spell. That should do the trick."

"Oh man, a spell!" Tank swooned. "You are my hero."

"Don't get ahead of yourself," Rufus scolded. "This is magic. It is nothing to be trifled with. Power can create wonderful, glorious sights. It can also produce paralyzing tragedies—or almost tragedies."

"Yeah." Mikey elbowed Tank. "Like that insane octopus. It could've killed someone."

"It could have," Rufus said.

Tank's gaze dropped to the ground, and Rufus placed a hand on his shoulder. "Listen, I know that you boys were only doing what you thought was right, that you weren't trying to hurt anyone. But there are consequences to all our actions."

"Including working magic?" Tank whispered.

"Especially working magic. It can have the gravest of consequences. But cheer up, we're here to stop the sprite from being able to do anything else bad. We're going to send it back to where it came from and we'll succeed."

"Because we've got good on our side?" Cory asked hopefully.

The innocence in his voice made my chest hurt. He was so sweet, so full of wonder. I didn't want to crap on his balloon.

"Yes," I told him, "because we've got good on our side."

Wasn't that how it was supposed to be? If goodness was working for you, you would prevail over evil, wouldn't you? At least thinking such a thing gave one hope. And hope was an important factor in life. Hope was what kept a person going; it's what kept them striving for a better life; it was what made people want to be better and to help others.

Hope was a thing that made the world go round.

Okay, so I might have been being a bit dramatic, but it was a big deal—at least to me.

I smiled at Rufus. "Come on. Let's put a dog to sleep and then do some spelunking."

He closed his eyes and grinned. "Of all the words that I never expected to hear come from your mouth, I'm fairly certain that 'spelunking' is at the top of the list."

I laughed. "Is it? Well, then I can *spelunk* all day long, if you'd like. Wait. Is that even a form of the word?"

"I don't believe so." He rubbed his hands together, charging the magic in the air. The atmosphere became thick, like humidity. You could almost cut through it with a knife. "Stand back, everyone. It's time for me to put this dog to sleep."

Rufus walked out from behind the hedge. The dog immediately saw him and started barking. It didn't even charge. But I supposed it didn't have to. When you're a big, strong dog full of big doggy testosterone, I supposed that you knew nothing could beat you and you weren't afraid of too much. So why bother charging or getting all snarly? There was no reason to.

I was pretty sure that was exactly how Mr. Rottweiler thought.

Anyway, Rufus parted his hands, and a blue light sprang from his palms. It surged toward the dog, which at that point actually did look a little frazzled before it doubled down on its whole attack-mode thing—which was to bark even more loudly than before.

Next thing I knew, the light had enveloped the creature and it had slumped to the ground, clearly out for the count.

"Well," I said, coming out from around the bush. "That was impressive."

"Man, that was so cool," Cory said, awestruck, as he pushed his bike across the yard. "Can you show me how to do that?"

"That took a lot of time to learn. I wasn't born with that sort of magic. Okay, I was. But I still had to learn how to wield certain spells and how to work them gently so that they wouldn't overpower anyone or hurt them."

"Yeah, I want to learn, too," Tank said. "That was so awesome."

"You guys are such dorks," Mikey replied.

"What?" Cory challenged. "You know you'd kill to be able to work magic like that. Why else do we play Dungeons and Dragons every Saturday?"

What had I said? They stayed inside on the weekends until their moms kicked them out.

Mikey didn't answer, probably because answering would have made him look desperate to know how to work the sort of magic that Rufus had worked. There wasn't anything desperate about that. Better to be honest than not. Heck, if I were them, I wouldn't have had any problem admitting that I wanted to be able to cast magic from my hands. Okay, I admit that throwing that spear had been way cool. I hadn't used power like that in a while, and it felt good.

Yes, I realized that I'd spent most of my life running from magic. But clearly it was here to stay, so I might as well get used to it.

Rufus told the boys that he'd work with them when it came to magic, and that really got them excited. Mikey even smiled, though I could tell he was trying to hide it as best he could.

We made our way across the yard. The boys had no problem locating the path that led down to the bottom of the bluff—and what a bluff it was.

Jagged rocks like teeth erupted from the side of the hill, the stones so sharp I didn't have to wonder if they would cut flesh or cloth because it was obvious. I shivered simply at the sight of them and was glad when we reached the forest floor.

A thick layer of leaves littered the ground. They were wet, as I supposed most forest floors that were canopied by trees were. My boots sank a bit as I walked, but the five of us had no problem keeping a swift pace as we trailed the wall to where the cavern was supposed to be.

"Most of the time," Mikey explained, "we come down here and find arrowheads and old pottery, stuff the natives left behind hundreds of years ago."

"We like to search for them," Cory explained. "One time I found an arrowhead this big." He split his hands about three inches. "It's on top of my dresser now."

"Very nice," Rufus said in a tone of congratulations. "The three of you must be good hunters."

"More like explorers," Tank countered. "That's how we like to think of ourselves—as kids who're exploring this area. No one else does, so we might as well."

"Sounds like y'all are the ones reaping the benefits," I said.

"That's right," Cory said. "At least, we thought that we were doing good until we called that creature. We're so sorry about that. Really. Do you think if the police find out it was us, they'll throw us into jail?"

The boys all gave one another a meaningful look. Ah, I got it now. They were, of course, worried about what they had done, the havoc that they had unleashed on Peachwood. But just like anybody, they were also concerned with their own butts. They wanted to make sure that their actions wouldn't hurt them.

"If we have to go to jail, we will," Mikey said. "We've already discussed it."

"Do you know what they do to kids like me in juvie," Tank lashed out. "I'll be dead meat."

"We'll be with you," Cory said. "We'll get your back. No one's going to hurt you, Tank, unless they come through us first."

"No one is going to jail," Rufus told them.

"They're not?" the boys said in unison, clearly confused but also a bit relieved.

"Absolutely not. What happened in the cave, you calling the sprite, it was an accident. However, it *was* the sprite that called the octopus and did so on purpose. That entire situation was a trap. The creature—the sprite, that is—wanted us to unleash that monster. If anyone is going to jail for destruction of property and putting people in absolute danger, it is the sprite, not the three of you."

Tank exhaled a sigh of relief. "Do you mean it?"

Anger flashed in Rufus's eyes. "I mean it."

His tone was curt, but he wasn't angry at the boys. He might have been at first, but that, I believe, quickly vanished as he spoke to them. The boys were nice. They were sweet. They weren't ruffians trying to destroy our town. They were simply boys—curious kids who played around with something that they shouldn't have. Sounded like the start of a movie called *Ouija*, if you wanted to know what I thought.

Not that I ever saw that movie. I didn't. But I mean, you don't have to have seen a movie like that to figure out what was going to happen. Kids messed with a Ouija board, they called a spirit that they were not supposed to—death and destruction occurred. The end.

Sounded pretty cut-and-dried to me.

"Here we are." Mikey leaned his bike against the bluff wall. "There's the opening to the cave."

It looked like a simple opening in a bluff. Dark smudges lined the ceiling, probably from campfires that had been set either by the natives or by kids just like these three.

Thank goodness they hadn't burned the forest to the ground.

The opening was tall enough for all of us to step into. It wasn't a deep crevice, just large enough for maybe a family to huddle up underneath the overhang to get out of weather.

"The cave's over here," Mikey told us.

We stepped into the very back of the cave, and I instantly spotted the rock that had been shoved aside. It had been clumsily put back into place, leaving a gap between the wall of the indentation in the bluff and the cavern it covered.

"We wiggled to get inside," Cory told us. "We had to tug on Tank a bit, too."

Tank blushed.

Rufus pushed the rock aside. "It's not large enough for me or Clem, which means I'll have to make it big enough."

"Are you gonna work more magic?" Tank asked, all mystified-like.

Rufus nodded. "Stand back, everyone. This may cause a bit of a rumble."

CHAPTER 20

Rufus pulled an orb from a sack on his back and studied it. "Yes, I think you'll do nicely."

But even when he said it, I sensed a bit of hesitancy. Was he one hundred percent certain that the particular spell he'd grabbed would do the trick? Or was he trying to convince himself more than he was trying to convince us?

I supposed that either way, time would tell.

He squished the orb between his fingers. I expected the magic to dart all over the place, to reach out and do what Rufus intended—for it to open the cave. But that wasn't what happened.

Instead, the orb soaked into his skin. Little fireworks of magic sparked on his fingertips. Rufus thrust out both hands, and the earth beneath our feet began to quake.

"Uh-oh," Mikey said. "We're in trouble now."

"We're not in trouble," Cory snapped. "Just watch."

Dirt and loose pebbles fell from the ceiling of the overhang as the cavernous mouth grew and grew and grew. The earth groaned and protested as its face opened.

I mean, it wasn't a face, but it sort of was.

Anyhow, the floor beneath our feet quaked and shook. It felt like the earth would open and swallow us whole. Just when I worried it might, the rumbling stopped.

Rufus wiped sweat from his brow. "There. I think that's tall enough for all of us."

"Do you think the inside's okay?" I asked. What if when Rufus opened the mouth of the cave, it collapsed something in the belly of darkness that we were about to enter? What if a gaping hole had opened just inside the yawning mouth? What if I plunged to my death? "Is it safe?"

Rufus plucked another orb from the sack. This one I recognized as a light orb. "I'm sending it on ahead."

He snapped his fingers, and the orb split into three. Rufus gave them a little push and they zipped inside the cavern, lighting the way ahead of us.

Good. That made me feel better.

We stepped inside. It was narrow, like you would expect a cave to be. There was simply something about tight, dark spaces that gave me the willies.

Perhaps it was the idea that if I was trapped in a place like that, there would be nowhere for me to run to, no place to escape. Where would I go? How would I manage to escape if, like, the ceiling fell in?

Why was I suddenly obsessed with a natural disaster occurring when I was about to walk right inside a place that could literally swallow me whole?

"Glad it's well lit," I murmured as I ducked my head into the hole.

And it was. The three orbs that Rufus had tossed into the cave made it glitter. Water leaked from an underground spring somewhere, leaving a trail of liquid down the face of one of the rocks.

I walked past the narrow opening and the cavern widened, allowing me to breathe. "Wow, it is way bigger inside than I expected."

"It is," Mikey added. "That's how come we explored."

"Yeah," Tank said, "it's pretty cool farther down."

We walked a little farther. The walls closed in again, and I had to hold my breath just to squeeze through a passage. But when I reached the other side, there sat a large pool of water and stalagmites that jutted from the earth, reaching to the ceiling, supporting it.

Or was that the other way around? Were they actually stalactites that ran from the ceiling to the floor? Either way, I didn't know.

"There's the book," Cory said.

By the pool sat what looked like a leather journal. Rufus plucked it from the ground. He brushed off the cover and unwound the leather cord wrapped around the body.

"This is someone's private magical book," he murmured. "A witch's, by what I can see. These are her spells, her personal collection." Rufus frowned. "But what's it doing here?"

I crossed to him and peered over his shoulder. "Perhaps this was where she worked her magic."

"Yeah," Mikey said. "I think it was—look!"

We glanced in the direction he pointed, and there we found an altar made of stones with old candles covering it. Wax dripped from the altar and spread to the floor. Old chalk lines had been drawn onto the rock floor as well.

"Don't touch anything," Rufus warned. "We don't know anything about this, who the witch was or what she was doing down here. Let me read for a moment."

The anger in Rufus's voice made the boys quiet. I thought they were beginning to see what Rufus had meant when he told them that playing with magic could have dangerous consequences. It wasn't simply working spells that you weren't familiar with, but even infiltrating a witch's or wizard's space could prove sticky. You didn't want to go erasing chalk lines that had been created for a reason. Who knew what havoc that could wreak? What if the chalk lines were keeping a demon at bay? If a person went and erased them, the demon could get loose.

That would have been bad. Very bad.

But anyway, Rufus scanned the book for a few minutes before saying solemnly, "This is a witch's journal, like I said. She had her own spell for calling a sprite. I found it. The traditional way to get rid of a sprite is to reverse the spell, say it backward entirely, but I'm not going to do that."

"Because of Lady." It wasn't a question. "You don't know how to turn her back."

"Right. So instead I'm going to muddy it."

"Muddy it?"

He nodded. "If I muddy the words, I'm thinking that I'll be able to weaken the sprite, then we can set a trap for it."

"My entire house inside is one big trap, in case you've forgotten."

He smiled. "I have not. But that trap didn't work, so we're going to do something else."

I pointed to the journal. "Do you think it's okay to take it?"

Rufus tucked it into the inside of his jacket pocket. "This place is abandoned. It hasn't been used for years. I'll return it when I'm done and will close up the cavern so that no one else will be able to read the spells ever again. There are some nasty ones in here. Not sure if they work, but if they did, our entire town would be in trouble." He shot the boys a hard look. "That means, in no uncertain terms, that the three of you are not allowed back in here ever again."

"But..." Tank started to argue, but his next words dissolved before even making it from his mouth. "All right. Will you teach us magic?"

"Yes," Rufus said flatly.

The boys gave each other high fives.

"On one condition," Rufus added.

They quieted. "What's that?" Cory asked.

"Whatever it is, I'm sure we'll do it," Mikey said.

Rufus wagged his finger sternly. "The condition is that before you ever even *think* of working a spell, you bring it to me first."

"Okay," they said together.

"All right." Rufus gave a hard nod. "Let's get out of here."

THE DOG WAS WAITING for us. Like, actually standing at the top of the bluff, looking down, patiently watching, waiting for us to reach the top.

We stood just on the bottom of the bluff, staring up. "Can you make it fall asleep again?" I asked.

Rufus opened his palm, but only a small trickle of magic fizzled from it. "I'm spent."

My jaw dropped. "You mean, you're out of magic?"

"Opening that cavern took a lot of it."

"But you used an orb," I argued.

He eyed me coolly, which meant he was annoyed by my question.

"Just because I used an orb doesn't mean that I didn't guide the magic myself, help it along. A lot of my power mingled with the energy to open that cavern."

I didn't know why I was so miffed. I guessed because there was supposed to be an endless supply of magic. Rufus wasn't supposed to run out. But even as that thought zipped through my head, I realized how ridiculous it sounded. Magic was like a muscle; there was only so much energy in it. Once that was used to exhaustion, it needed to recover. But why had Rufus's magic chosen to sputter out at that exact moment, when we needed it to get past a dog that looked like it would enjoy eating all of us for its lunch?

I folded my arms and said to Rufus, "Do you think that you could find more magic hidden somewhere?"

"You really don't understand the words, 'I'm out of magic,' do you?"

"I just think that you're not digging deep enough."

He chuckled. "Tell you what, I might be able to find more."

"Good. Great. That was all I wanted to hear. Right, boys?"

They mumbled something but mostly looked away. I didn't think they enjoyed watching two people argue. Rufus and I probably shouldn't have been arguing to begin with, but, rabid dog and all.

Didn't that explain it?

Rufus took my hands. "I'll guide your magic."

"Huh? What are you talking about?" And that wasn't what he was supposed to have said. My boyfriend was supposed to have said that he would find a way to work *his* magic, not manipulate mine. I hadn't signed up for that in the deal. "How will you guide my magic?"

"Simple. I'll feed what's left of mine into yours and will guide it. I'll show you how to put the dog to sleep. All I need for you to do is relax, have an open mind." When I didn't say anything, he added, "I know this is hard for you, but pretend that it's easy and it will be."

I wasn't going to admit it was hard or that I was uncertain about any of it, because I wanted to get by that dog in one piece. I also didn't want to be chased down by a man with a shotgun for being on his property illegally.

I turned to the boys. "What do y'all normally do in this situation?"

Mikey shrugged. "We haven't had this situation before. The dog's usually not waiting for us."

Great. Of course the Rottweiler had to be different today of all days. Seeing as there was no other way out of this, I said, "Okay, Rufus. I'm your pallet. Do with me what you will."

He chuckled. "You act as if I'm taking over your mind. I'm only guiding your magic. This won't hurt too much."

I reeled back. "Who said anything about it hurting? I'm not signing up for that."

"I'm joking. Give me your hand, and let your magic flow."

"How do I…?"

"Shh. Concentrate."

I closed my eyes. How was I supposed to let my magic flow? Whenever I'd used it before, it had always been in stressful situations. At least, I thought it had. Not that I was counting. I wasn't counting. So I had no idea what he meant by just *concentrate.*

Oh, right. *There* was a nudge. I felt a push as if someone was poking me in the stomach. But when I glanced down at my naval, Rufus wasn't poking me.

He was prodding me with his magic. I whispered, "What am I supposed to do?"

He'd closed his eyes but opened one a slit. "Let me in."

He said it as if it was so obvious. Well, it wasn't obvious to me.

"It will help if you close your eyes."

"Oh, okay."

I closed my eyes and waited for something to happen. I could still feel his magic poking me, and honestly, it was almost getting a little annoying. What was with all the prodding?

I was about to say as much, but then suddenly I inhaled and exhaled, and felt myself fall into a deep moment of concentration. Do you know what? My magic opened like a flower, and it let his power in.

What the heck?

Our magics intertwined, intermingled. It was sexy, y'all. It wasn't just my magic that opened up, I felt *myself* open up to Rufus. Like, my entire body was suddenly this rose that was unfurling and ready for action.

Sorry. That was probably way too much information. But it was strange and cool and wonderful. His magic circled around me like a ribbon, teasing me, and my magic snapped back at it playfully.

And then, just when I was really starting to enjoy the sensation, Rufus murmured, "Now tame it and make it yours."

Oh, okay. Like I knew how to do that. But somehow I did. My magic wound around his, and the two different lines melted together, becoming one.

It was smexy.

"Now," he whispered heavily (he might have been feeling all smexy, too), "think about sleep and send it into the dog."

"That's all?" I had to force the words out because I was still very enchanted with the whole feeling that I'd been under. "Nothing else?"

"Nothing else."

With my eyes still closed and my entire body buzzing with energy, I pictured the dog asleep and tossed our magic up and out to the creature.

I heard a thump and opened my eyes.

Mikey and boys clapped. "You did it!"

I smiled at Rufus. "Thank you! We did it!"

His cheeks were on fire they were so red. "You did well."

My own cheeks were smoldering, too. I smiled bashfully (I don't know why I suddenly felt so embarrassed). "All right. Let's get home and work on the next stage of the plan."

Rufus started up the hill, replying, "I couldn't have said it better myself."

CHAPTER 21

We tried to get rid of the boys. Or at least, I thought that Rufus was attempting to send them home when he said, "Thanks for your help, kids. You've done a lot."

"We plan on seeing this through to the end," Tank said.

The end? Like, until the sprite was gone? That sort of end?

"It's dangerous," Rufus explained.

Cory shrugged. "We're used to danger. After all, we had to avoid that dog to reach the bluff."

"Yeah, and we're tough," Mikey added. "We know what we need to be men."

Tank and Cory didn't miss a beat. They nodded seriously. I had to bite my lip to keep from laughing.

"Well, being a man means admitting when you're wrong," Rufus said. "And you've all done that."

"That's why we want to be there when you catch the sprite," Tank replied with gusto. "We want to make sure that it gets sent back to wherever it came from."

Rufus glanced at me, and I gave a slight shrug. The kids had a point. If they wanted to be present when we captured the sprite, perhaps it would have been best if they were. They kind of deserved it. After all, they hadn't been forced to come forward and explain that they were the cause of the sprite's appearance in town. But they had on their own accord. To me, that had said a lot about their character—or *characters*, as it were, since there were three of them.

"Maybe we should let them help." It was getting cold, and I zipped up my coat. "As long as they stay far enough away that they don't get hurt, I don't see why they can't be a part of the next steps."

Rufus's face pinched. I could tell that he was thinking he didn't want the kids anywhere near the next phase of the plan, whatever that was, but he also knew that the boys had started this whole thing and they should be there to end it, too.

At least, that was what I thought he was thinking.

"Okay," he relented, but I could tell he was not too happy about it. "You can help capture the sprite." The boys cheered in celebration, but Rufus's voice cut them off. "But if one of you disobeys me, in *anything*, even something as simple as where I tell you to stand, you're all out. Is that clear?"

A round of *yes sirs,* came from them. I smiled at Rufus. His mouth quirked. He almost looked amused at how serious the boys were.

"Good," he told them. "Now. Let's get to Clementine's house, and we'll go over the plan."

The boys tossed their bikes into the back of my pickup, which I'd driven over to the neighborhood that housed the bluff. They got into the bed of the truck, and Rufus and I climbed into the cabin.

As I cranked her up, I said, "Do you think they'll mind?"

"They'd better," he said darkly. "Their very lives could depend on it."

As soon as we pulled onto the street, Malene was storming down her front porch, binoculars swinging from her neck. Urleen and Norma Ray followed. It didn't take too much brain power to figure out that they'd been waiting for us—or *on* us, for something.

"What took y'all so long?" Malene demanded after I'd parked.

Rufus stepped out of the vehicle. "We had to enlarge the mouth of a cave, put a vicious Rottweiler to sleep and then do the same thing on the way back. We've had a day."

"So have we," Norma Ray said. "The phone's been blowing up all afternoon. Everyone heard about the giant octopus, and they're all worried."

My heart seized. "Has anyone seen the sprite? Has it acted up again?"

"Not that we know of," Urleen remarked, gesturing for us to go inside. "But there's no telling what will happen next."

Rufus paused. He studied the landscape of houses as if waiting for one of them to talk. "It's waiting. The sprite is waiting for the perfect moment to strike. Come on, boys. Let's go inside and we'll come up with a plan."

We found Lady waiting impatiently inside the house. Chocolate was smeared all over her face. When she saw me, she rushed up and pawed at my arms. "Thank goodness you're back. And you brought my stepdaddy!"

The entire room went quiet. The last thing that I wanted to do was look back and see how Rufus was reacting to being called *stepdaddy*, but I also had to know. It was like being witness to a train wreck happening right in front of your eyes. You didn't want to look, but you just had to. Something about the wreck just wouldn't allow you to look away.

And when I peeked at Rufus, his cheeks were tinged burnt sienna. He'd gone from red to straight-up crimson brown in color.

His blood pressure must've been through the roof. I gathered that it was not the right time to tell him that Lady called him her stepdaddy.

I did my best to play the whole potential fiasco off. "Stepdaddy? What are you talking about? There's nobody like that here."

"Oh, was I not supposed to say that? But I call Rufus my stepdaddy all the time."

This just got worse and worse.

But wouldn't you know it, it was Rufus who saved the day. He smiled kindly. "You can refer to me as that. In fact, I'm honored that you think of me that way, Lady."

"Wait," Tank said, "is she your daughter?" He pointed to me. "Are you *that* old?"

By which he meant, was I old enough to have a grown-up daughter? Oh, how I hated kids and their inability to judge a person's age. To them, everyone was forty or older. I didn't want to ask them how old they thought I was. They would probably say something stupid like fifty.

And then I would have to murder them.

Just kidding.

Not really.

"I knew you wouldn't mind if I called you stepdaddy," Lady said smugly. "I'd told Clem that, but she didn't listen."

"Can we just get on with the plan?" I asked. "And not keep talking about this?"

Because the more we talked about it, the more embarrassed it made me.

We all took seats in the living room. Well, the women did. The boys and Rufus stood.

"Now that we're all here, we have a problem," Malene said.

"Tell us," Rufus stated.

Malene's gaze swished to her friends. "Well, um, now that the whole town knows about the octopus, they're worried. It wasn't so bad when I just told them that they needed to be on the lookout for a sprite, but someone"—she gave Norma Ray a cold look—"decided they needed to know every tiny detail about what had happened today."

"They should know," Rufus said. "They deserve the truth. The more they know, the better. There is a potential for real danger here, as we've seen."

Urleen cleared her throat. "The problem is, these people are expecting results and they're expecting them fast. If they don't get them…"

When she stopped talking, I asked, "If they don't get them, what? What will they do?"

"They plan to come over here and demand that Rufus leave," Malene said.

My jaw dropped. "What? Why would they demand that?"

"Because someone heard about his past and they've been spreading it like wildfire."

"Who?" I asked.

"Henrietta," Urleen said flatly. "That's who."

"That nice woman?" I couldn't believe it. She was going to make my boyfriend leave town because of his past? Well, I wasn't going to let that happen. I would have a talk with her. This nonsense would stop. "We'll see about that."

"I told you to watch out for Presbyterians." Malene pursed her lips proudly because she'd been right about something. "Now you know why. They all seem nice until they stab you in the back. Now you know why I had to cheat to win the art competition."

"You cheated?" Cory asked.

Oh no. Geriatric cheating was not a good look on Malene. It was also not a good influence on impressionable boys.

"She's only joking," I said quickly. "Don't mind her."

"I didn't know that adults cheated," Mikey said, mystified.

"They *don't*," I told him. "There was no cheating. She was only joking. Tell him, Malene."

But Malene said not one word. That made me want to jump up and strangle the truth right out of her, and I wasn't even a violent person.

I fleetingly wondered if I could use a little magic to influence her. But before I had a chance to explore that option, Rufus broke in.

"If all of that is happening in town, then we need a plan to deal with the sprite, and fast. The good news is, we have the incantation that called it. The bad news is, we have to capture the creature. We can't simply banish it. We need it to put Lady back to normal, and then we'll banish it back to where it came from."

"So we need a trap," Urleen mused.

"Not just any trap, a good one," Rufus corrected. "When I use the spell, the sprite will probably appear near us, but there's no way to predict with one hundred percent accuracy where it will show up."

"Will it be visible?" I asked.

He shrugged. "Another unknown."

We were all silent for a moment. I was deep in thought, trying to figure something out. We could always lure it to my house and then throw a blanket on it. But how could we lure it? And how would we know that it was nearby? When I'd dropped flour on it, I'd been able to track the creature and its movements.

"We could always…" Malene said, then paused. "No, never mind."

"What about…?" Norma Ray shook her head. "Forget it. It'll never work."

What if we put a huge amount of flour in a big sack and then suspended it from a tree? When the sprite walked underneath it, we could dump the flour on top of it!

But then how would we know the sprite was beneath the flour. Wait! We could dust the ground with the stuff, too. But what if the sprite was too smart for that?

Then my mind started really working, but unfortunately nothing was coming to me. I was mostly thinking about how hungry I was and how I could use some chocolate pie.

"If only we had something it wanted," Rufus said quietly.

It hit me. "I do!" I jumped up from my chair. How could I have forgotten about it? Well, what with Lady being a human and fighting a big octopus, it wasn't surprising that I'd been a touch distracted. "I've got something the sprite wants. Y'all stay right here, and I'll go get it."

CHAPTER 22

We had the plan all set, but we weren't going to enact it until later, when it was dark. For some reason, Rufus, Malene and her gang thought it would be best to set the trap after nightfall because then the sprite would be confused since it wasn't daylight. Or it would be easier to disorient it, I supposed.

Here was the thing—I thought we could catch the critter better during the day. I thought—and rightly so, I figured—that we'd be able to see it, and because we could see it, we'd have a better shot at apprehending it.

But no one else saw things that way—especially not the boys, who all said they'd have to sneak out of their houses after supper to come help.

I had thought we were trying to shape those young men to do good, not encourage them into being juvenile delinquents. But anyway, apparently my opinion was in the minority, because everyone voted that we would put plan Catch That Sprite into action after supper.

On the upside, that did give me some time to run around a little bit downtown. I had a few items on my food shopping list, and since my pantry was empty thanks to one mischievous sprite, I needed to do some restocking.

I reached downtown soon enough and quickly found myself shopping for everything *except* what I'd come to look for. It was hard to stay focused on food when there were pretty things right in front of my eyes —things like cabinetry and lamps.

I really, really enjoyed making houses look good, y'all. A bit too much, some would say.

But anyway, just as I was turning away from an antique store that had a beautiful buffet that was way too big for my dining room but I really wanted to buy it just so that I could put it in there anyway, I bumped into Lance from Architectural Scavengers.

"Lance, how're you?"

"Oh, Clem," he said, sounding and looking distressed, "I'm not good at all."

"Why not? What happened?"

"Right after you left the store the other day, I suddenly couldn't find my wallet. I've been looking everywhere for it—underneath furniture, on top of things. But I can't find it. I know that I didn't take it out of my pocket when you were in the shop, but do you remember seeing it lying around?"

"No," I said sadly, "I don't."

I thought back quickly to that day and what had occurred. I had an idea—a strange one, one that might have even sounded half crazy, but also one that I was sure to be correct.

Actually I wasn't sure that I was right, but I had an idea that there were two thieves in Peachwood—one was a sprite and one was human. But the human wasn't committing the thefts intentionally.

I realized that by saying all of that, I wasn't giving much away, but just hang with me; we'll get there.

"Lance," I said, trying to erase that worried look on his face, "I think I might know what happened. If you give me a little bit of time, I'll be able to prove it. I just can't do it today."

At first he looked excited, but when I said that I wouldn't be able to help him that day, the dejected expression filled his face again.

"It's not that I don't want to," I added quickly. "It's just that there's something really important that I need to do. But don't worry. I don't think anything's been stolen from your wallet."

"That's the funny thing," he admitted. "None of my credit cards have been used."

"Right. That's what I thought. Okay, first thing tomorrow, I'll explain everything. But for now, you have to trust me. And I've got to get some food because I've got a sprite to catch later tonight."

He reeled back. "A sprite? Oh my goodness, I didn't know you were mixed in with all this mess. Henrietta has just about gone and lost her mind. She's thinking of kicking out the one wizard who can save us all —and who also happens to be quite handsome," he added with a wink.

Heat rushed up my cheeks. "Tell me about it. We're planning a trip to Fiji."

He gave me a cool once-over. "Well, you might want to leave the bikini at home and take lots of tanning oil."

I barked a laugh. "Stop it. We're going to get away, not to enjoy some honeymoon that we won't even be having."

He shrugged. "If you say so."

"I do say so."

"Well, be sure to do lots of things that I would do," he said with a wink, which made me laugh and blush once again.

"Now, now. You know that I'm a good girl."

"You can't be too good if you're going gallivanting off with a wizard to Fiji."

"Well, you know, it's Fiji and all."

"Can't say I blame you there. But look, call me first thing in the morning and let me know what you do. I'll be waiting with bated breath."

"I will; I promise."

We air-kissed each other's cheeks, and I left. I did eventually get some food and headed back to the house. As soon as I was through the door, Lady was accosting me.

"It's about time you returned. I'm starving. What do you think, I can live on air?"

"You've survived on ice cream for breakfast, so I have no doubt you'll be able to find something."

"The ice cream's all gone," she confessed, gaze darting to the ground.

My eyes widened. "All of it? There was nearly an entire half gallon in that container."

She cringed. "I know, but I was hungry. You know me, Clem! I have a huge appetite! I've been stressed, so I've been eating even more! I'm so ashamed of myself. Please forgive me." She dropped to her knees and took my hands, sniffing them. "Do I smell hot dogs?"

"Um, maybe. Stop sniffing my hands. That is gross. You're a human. Humans don't sniff one another's hands. They don't sniff hands or butts or faces or anything like that."

"But I am a dog," she howled. "And I cain't help it!" Lady paused. "But *do* you have hot dogs?"

"Yes. Get up off the floor, and I'll make you one."

"Or two or three."

Good thing she wasn't going to be human for very much longer (I hoped), because with the way Lady was scarfing down food, she'd grow two or three pant sizes in a week.

As I fixed the hot dogs, Lady talked to me. "I know that I'm going to become a dog soon, but isn't it fun having girl chat, Clem?"

What in the world was she talking about? "Um. Yeah. Great."

"I mean, don't you love just hanging out like girlfriends and talking about boys and doing our nails and hair?"

I slid a couple of hot dogs into the toaster oven. "First of all, we talked when you were a dog. Secondly, we haven't once done our nails and hair since you've been human."

She curled her hands around her knee. "But wouldn't it be fun to?"

"I don't think so. As soon as I painted your nails, you'd probably ruin them by scratching at the door to go out so that you could pee in the front yard."

"You know, I may keep this whole toilet thing going after I turn back."

"You can't reach it," I reminded her.

"All you have to do is get me a little doggy stool. Then I'd be able to climb onto the toilet. Just get me one of those kid-sized seats that goes on top of the full-sized one, and I'll be fine."

I frowned. "How do you know about kid-sized seats?"

"I watch TV, Clem. There ain't nothing else to do around here."

"Oh yeah, right." The toaster oven dinged that the dogs were done. I plated them and added a handful of potato chips onto each dish and placed both on the table. "Supper is served."

"It's too bad my stepdaddy couldn't make it."

"Rufus had other things to do tonight. He had to prepare his spells."

"Why didn't he ask you to join him?"

"He knew that I had you to take care of, so he didn't want to burden me with anything else. Besides. He can do it—get everything ready. That sort of thing. No problem."

And it wasn't a problem. It had been a long day for us both, and Rufus had explicitly told me to get some rest before tonight so that I'd be ready.

Of course, I hadn't gotten any rest. I'd gone out shopping, and now I was about to be talked to death by Lady.

"Well, are you ready?" she asked.

No. "Yes, I'm the most ready that I ever could be. Don't even think I'm not, because I am ready to take that sucker out."

Was I? I felt that I was. Sort of. There were a lot of things that could potentially go wrong. There were also a lot that could go right.

I was praying that everything would go right and be, well, *right*, I guessed.

"Well, I ain't worried," Lady said briskly. Almost too briskly. "I know that we're gonna win over this devil. We are gonna get him thrown back to where he belongs, and that's going to be the end of it."

"I'm sure it will all work out."

But something was worming around in my stomach. I didn't know if it was foreshadowing or dramatic irony or something else that I couldn't name. Either way, I had the sinking feeling that this plan would go really, really wrong.

But just as I was thinking that, my phone rang. "Hello?"

"Clem," Rufus replied in a low, gravelly voice that was full of loads of confidence and darkness. Don't ask me how a voice could be dark, but Rufus was a pro at it.

"Yes?" I asked, nearly breathless from all the dark edginess in his tone.

"It's time. I'll meet you out front."

I gulped. It was showtime.

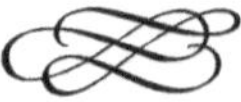

e were all in position. Rufus had wanted us to pick a quiet place, nothing that would be too busy with people. Of course, Malene volunteered our street. The way she saw it, with her, me and Willard out of our homes and working to catch the sprite, that would mean the block would already be half-empty.

"Safest place in town," she'd said.

Rufus had agreed. I had not. After all, if another giant octopus appeared, it might crush my house. I didn't think State Farm would consider that an act of God in my insurance coverage. That would probably go under the line *freak accident,* for which I was certain there was no policy on record.

The short explanation was that I would be screwed.

But there was no telling Malene that.

Anyhoo, Mikey, Tank and Cory were set up behind a row of cars. Their job was to throw a net on the sprite at the right time. They weren't supposed to touch it or interact with it other than that. Rufus had been explicit in his directions. Basically he wanted to keep the boys safe.

They also wanted to stay safe since Rufus had promised them wizarding lessons, which the three were practically salivating over.

Malene, Urleen and Norma Ray had one job and one job only—to ensure that the sack of flour fell on the sprite at the right time. Those three huddled behind a big red oak, waiting for the moment to release the bag.

They reminded me of the teenagers in *Carrie*, waiting to drop the bucket of pig's blood on her head. I prayed that the sprite didn't go all Carrie on us and destroy my entire town.

But that was what Rufus was for. The reason why he wasn't in charge of the flour or corralling the sprite was because he oversaw the magic part of the evening. He had to work the spell, make sure that he said it backward to call the sprite to us. If his concentration broke, the spell would break and who knew the badness that would happen then. The sprite could simply become enraged and start shooting rockets down the street.

So, Rufus had to be able to focus.

The only two folks left were me and Lady. Our job, our single purpose was to identify when the sprite appeared. I would in essence be bait, holding onto the sprite's tie that I had. Surely the creature would want its tie back. I meant, it could have wanted it. If it was wearing an outfit and the outfit didn't work without that particular ebony color and cut of fabric, then yes, the sprite was going to want its accessory.

At least, I hoped so. After all, I never forgot a great accessory.

But then again, I wasn't a sprite.

Lady was with me, in the hopes of grabbing the sprite's attention. If he remembered changing her from a dog into a human, that was. And we were betting on that. If the tie didn't lure the sprite in, maybe Lady would.

So Lady and I were standing just outside the flour ring's trajectory. Once the flour dumped onto the sprite, the boys would jump into action with the net. Then Rufus would coerce the sprite into changing Lady back, and he would finish the spell and banish the sprite for good.

Or so we hoped.

Rufus eyed all of us. It was a nearly unreadable expression, but I saw the fire lit in that gaze. My boyfriend was determined to end this and to get everything right the first time.

"Everyone ready?" he asked.

We all nodded.

"Then let's begin."

It was solemn work. Rufus began the chant, and I felt the hairs on the back of my head rise.

"Oh, I've got the willies," Lady said with a shiver.

"It's the magic. It's powerful."

"Feels old, like some old witch with bad skin made this her life's work because she was too ugly to get a man."

"That is a terrible thing to say," I whispered.

"Hey, if the shoe fits," she explained.

"You don't know if the shoe fit."

"I do. I'm sure of it."

Rather than argue a moot point with her (obviously we would never know if the witch who'd created the book was ugly or not), I simply kept my mouth shut and watched and waited—all while holding out the tie.

As Rufus spoke, the wind changed. It shifted direction, whipping my hair so hard that it slapped my face. Having my skin sting because of my hair wasn't exactly what I called a good time.

Wish I'd had the foresight to pull it back.

Just as I was thinking that, something tugged on the tie. It was like when you've cast a fishing line and you feel the pull of a fish as it nibbles the bait, deciding if what you're offering is worth sinking its teeth into.

"The sprite," I shouted. "It's here!"

"Where?" Lady asked, gesturing.

Her hand moved wildly, flailing as if it wasn't attached to her body. Granted, she'd only been human a couple of days, so she wasn't exactly used to her appendages. Her hand hit my hand, the one holding onto the tie.

The tie loosened in my grip…and was snatched out from my grasp.

"No," I shouted as Malene released the flour. Lady and I stepped forward and suddenly got doused with the stuff.

But it wasn't just us who got covered. The sprite was still within reach. It got covered as well, coated in a layer of white powder.

I was able to clearly see it. The creature was ugly, though humanlike, with a long, fat nose and rounded cheeks. Its eyes narrowed at me as I lunged for it.

"Now," Mikey yelled.

The boys tossed the net, but they didn't throw it far enough. The sprite saw them coming and darted away. The net, weighted on the ends, sailed in the air and came down on top of mine and Lady's heads.

"It's run off," Lady screamed. "The sprite's loose."

Rufus stopped chanting. His gaze latched onto the sprite, who was clearly still visible as it zipped down the street, leaving a trail of flour in its wake.

Rufus threw an orb (I had no idea that he was even holding one). It landed just in front of the sprite and became a red gelatinous mound, like someone had dropped a dumpster truck of Jell-O on the street.

Oh, the neighbors were going to hate us after this.

The sprite ran right into the mound, which held it like cement. Without waiting a moment, Rufus was gone, dashing down the street.

"Let's get this net off," I said.

Lady and I struggled to get the net off our heads. At the same time, a car whipped down the street and parked. Henrietta got out, pointed to Rufus and shouted, "There he is! The man who needs to be kicked out of Peachwood!"

Oh no! She'd awaken the entire neighborhood. But she wasn't alone. Out of the car stepped three other grannies holding rolling pins.

Rolling pins? Were they going to bake off? Or was bludgeoning a man over the head their idea of vigilante justice?

I had the feeling the latter was the right option.

The boys helped Lady and me get the net off us just as Rufus reached the sprite. I didn't wait for anybody to give me permission to go—I ran and ran fast. I charged straight toward the melee as Henrietta pulled her own rolling pin from her jacket and raised it like a weapon against Rufus.

"Rufus," I shouted in case he hadn't seen the object of death coming for him. He did, but not quite in time. He jerked out of the way as the pin grazed the side of his head.

I grimaced as the object made contact. He reeled back, struck by Henrietta and whatever insanity had gotten into her.

Meanwhile the sprite was struggling in the Jell-O. I had to reach it, had to stop it before it escaped. Henrietta raised her hand to give Rufus another wallop, and I screamed, "No!"

I threw my hand out, not thinking, not attempting to do anything.

All I knew that I wanted was for her not to hit Rufus again. I wanted her to leave him alone, and for good.

Just as that thought entered my head, the rolling pin flew from her hand and sailed through the sky. I exhaled a gust of air and pointed at the three other rolling pins. They too, sailed into the sky, never to be seen or heard from again.

I was just kidding. I was sure they would be found, but hopefully by a more sane baker who wanted to use the pins to actually roll out dough as opposed to hitting helpful wizards that I loved over the skull.

Anyhow, I reached Rufus, put my arms on his shoulders and shouted at the women, "How dare you? He's trying to help the situation, not make it worse. You're the ones who are going to make it worse, by hurting him. Do you know what you could have done?"

They stared at me, slack-jawed, but I wasn't finished. "You could have caused a huge catastrophe in this town. If you thought that monster was bad—and I'm not admitting that there was a monster—but if you thought it was bad, then you haven't seen anything yet. Because that sprite"—who was currently coated in flour and attempting to swim through a rock of Jell-O—"is nothing if not a prankster. He's the one who stole the food in your church's pantry, same as he did to us. He is the cause of all these problems, and by hurting Rufus, you would let the sprite loose to wreak even more havoc. Honestly, just because you aren't witches doesn't mean that all witches and wizards are bad. Can you please just get a grip?" I glanced at Rufus. "Are you okay?"

"I'm okay, just a little dizzy."

"You probably gave him a concussion," I hissed at Henrietta. "And here I thought you were a nice person. That wasn't a nice thing to do at all. It was mean and—"

"Clem," Rufus said.

"Yes?"

"The sprite."

"Oh, right."

The creature was struggling so hard inside the Jell-O that it had managed to nearly claw/swim its way to the other side. It was nearly out of the entire mound.

No! It was going to get free!

Just as panic mode was about to settle into my chest, Lady darted up with the net. "Thought y'all might want this," she said smugly, because of course my dog knew that we would need a net. She had some sort of sixth sense about her.

I raced in front of the mound, and just as the sprite was about to lurch out and scamper away, I wrangled the net around its body and captured it!

Hooray for me!

But the sprite wasn't very pleased. That creature started spitting and scratching and cussing. Boy, it had a foul mouth. I would not have wanted to be the mother who got kissed with those lips. Disgusting.

"Stop it," I scolded. "Just stop it. No one here wants to harm you. No one wants to hurt you, so will you just stop struggling?"

Henrietta peered close and then reared back. "What in the world is that?"

"That," came Malene's voice, "is the sprite who's been causing all the problems in our town. That's the creature who stole your jewels."

She clutched her throat. "It did?"

As Malene gave a self-satisfied nod, I interjected, "Actually it's not. I don't think it was responsible for those thefts. But I know who was, and I'm planning to fix that tomorrow."

"Tomorrow?" Henrietta looked appalled at such an idea. "Why not today?"

"Because today we have to banish a sprite." Rufus winced as he brought his fingers away from the spot where Henrietta had walloped him. "So if you don't mind, would you please give us some room?"

The sprite was still cussing up a storm as Henrietta and her friends took a slight step back. Everyone stared at the flour-coated creature in wonder, especially the boys, who whispered among themselves. I couldn't hear what; all I could make out were the sounds of *pssss, pspsp-sps, psspsp.*

You know, whisper noises.

It was distracting.

Rufus hushed the sprite. "No one here is going to harm you. Would you calm down a moment?" The sprite still cussed up a storm. "We're going to send you home. There. Will you stop cursing us so that I can speak to you?"

The sprite finally shut its trap.

A look crossed Rufus's face that said, *There, was that so hard?* But of course he didn't say that. It probably would've just made the sprite mad again.

"We're sorry that you were called here," Rufus started. "Bringing you here was a mistake, one that I'm about to correct. But I need you to do something first."

The sprite didn't answer. Rufus waved a hand over it, and some magical dust fell from his fingertips. In an instant the sprite was clean, and he was very visible.

I grimaced. The creature had what folks called, a face for radio, or a face only a mother could love. It was very ugly with a bulbous nose and its mouth curled into a snarl.

"Stop staring at me, you ugly beasts," he said.

It was definitely a *he.* The sprite's voice was deep, and it wore a little suit. But wait. Who was it calling ugly beasts? We weren't ugly. I wasn't ugly. Lady wasn't. Perhaps beauty was in the eye of the beholder. In that case, the sprite was a big old beholder.

"We apologize for staring," Rufus said gently. "But I need you to work one last bit of magic before I send you back."

The sprite's gaze washed up and down him skeptically. "What?"

He nodded to Lady. "Turn her back into a dog."

The sprite laughed—actually threw its head back and chuckled. "You don't like her the way she is?"

"No," I said flatly. "She's a dog. Please turn her back. Look, we're sorry that you're here. We're sorry that we interrupted your life and took you away from your family and friends." Er—did it have family and friends? It was best just to go with that, I figured. "And we want you to return to them, but we don't know how to change her back. Only you do. Please."

The sprite exhaled. "I didn't want to be here," he grumbled. "And I was very hungry."

So it *ate* all the food it stole? Wow. What an appetite.

"And you"—he gave me a sharp look that made me wither—"stole my tie."

"I didn't steal it, you left it in one of the churches that you took food from," I snapped. "Then you turned my dog into a human."

"Well you tried to trap me," he shot back.

Oh, he was right, there. We had booby-trapped my house. "Sorry," I admitted.

He hmphed. "Fine. I'll turn her back." The sprite wiggled his eyebrows, and the next thing I knew, Lady had shrunk and returned to being a dog.

Thank goodness.

"What's everybody staring at?" she snarled. "Ain't none of y'all ever seen a dog before?"

I scooped her into my arms. "We're all just glad you're back to the way you're supposed to be."

"Does this mean I cain't eat chocolate no more?"

"Yes, it does."

"Drat."

Rufus started chanting again. Magic whirled all around the sprite, enveloping him in a cloud of pixie dust. "'Bout time I get to go home," he said.

Good riddance to him, too.

We all watched as the magic tightened and squeezed the sprite. At first I was afraid it was going to harm him, but I relaxed when the creature's hand shot out and he flipped us the bird.

Such a charming creature.

A few seconds later the cloud disappeared and the sprite with it. All of us exhaled.

Norma Ray spoke. "I'm glad that's over."

Henrietta winced. "I'm sorry for hitting you."

"It's okay," Rufus said graciously.

"Thank you for saving our town," she said. The other women thanked him, too.

We were all tired and worn. But I was the same as them, grateful that the night was over and that the sprite had been sent to live back with its own sprite people.

Rufus gave me a lopsided smile. "You ready to call it a night?"

I wrapped my arm around his waist and peered up at him. "Readier than I'll ever be."

CHAPTER 24

The next few days saw life getting back to normal in Peachwood. Henrietta called off the charge to get rid of Rufus. For that, I was grateful. It almost made me realize something—even though Henrietta was a sweet person, when she was pushed into a corner, she wanted what everyone else wanted, to protect her friends.

Since she had thought Rufus was the cause of our problems—you know, wizard in town and all that—she figured getting rid of him would end those problems as well.

Well, that was the wrong way of thinking, and she realized it, for which I was glad.

Which leads me to her jewels and the other objects missing from town, like Lance's wallet.

All of that got solved with one trip to Bender's coffee shop.

I'd just paid for a coffee and chocolate doughnut and was heading out of the store when Jessica entered. Spotting her, I pulled the newcomer to town aside.

"Gosh, did you hear that whole thing about the octopus?" I asked her.

Jessica's eyes widened to plates. "I did. You don't think it was real, do you?"

I smiled. "It was real. I'm sorry to say. When you came to Peachwood, you didn't bet on living in a magical town, did you? In fact, I've been hearing that lots of people who didn't have magic before are coming into their own."

Her gaze darted to the ground. "Um, yeah."

"Jessica, it's okay if you have magic. I think you do, don't you? Some sort of disappearing magic that you're not sure how to control."

Her eyes filled with tears. "I'm so sorry. I didn't mean to take those things. I didn't even know that I had. They were just in my purse when I looked." She opened her bag, and there sat Henrietta's jewelry and Lance's wallet. "I wanted to return everything, but I didn't want to be arrested for taking these thing."

I smiled and placed a hand over her arm. "You won't be. I know it was an accident. Come on. I know just the person who can help you."

We returned the objects, and I introduced her to Rufus later that day, explaining that he was going to have to start a magical school to help all the new witches and wizards learn how to handle their magic.

He grumbled something, which made me think he wasn't quite as convinced as I was about the use of such a school. But we would see.

Malene did eventually admit that she'd cheated in the art competition (after she found her ribbon tucked into a cushion of her couch—wonder how it got there). Mac had been sad but apparently not surprised.

"I wondered how you'd suddenly gotten so much talent," he said when she admitted it.

That was what Malene told me. So I actually had no way of knowing if it was true.

But anyway, she did hand over her blue ribbon, which was then given to Henrietta, who handed it back to Malene, telling her that she deserved it for all she'd done to help save Peachwood from the sprite.

So in the end, Malene wound up with the blue ribbon after all. She swore that never again would she cheat at anything.

Not sure if I believed her, but time would tell. Now, wouldn't it?

Lady's life returned to normal. Though she said that she missed being human, she seemed content enough to be a dog, enjoying our nights when she'd curl up beside me and lay her head on my arm.

No, I don't think she missed being a person too much. Being a dog had way too many benefits, if you asked me.

And as for me...well, my life got back to the same old, same old. Rufus and I were planning our trip. In fact, there was a witch in town who he told me had been to Fiji recently, and he wanted me to meet her.

"Are you sure Mikey, Tank and Cory will allow you to take a night off?"

Rufus barked a laugh. "They're very demanding, those three. Love to learn about magic. They want to soak every bit of knowledge from me that they can."

"Well, as long as they leave the important parts," I told him. "I don't want too much of you being sucked away."

He laughed again and wrapped an arm around my shoulders. "You don't have to worry about that."

We were out for a walk. He'd told me that the witch didn't live far from him, and we were just going to pop on by. "Ah, here's the house."

It was a small cottage painted green with gray shutters. A rope of ivy twisted its way across the porch, making the home look, well, homey.

Rufus squeezed my hand. "She's got a lot of information. You'll want to hear it all."

"I can't wait," I nearly squealed. After dealing with the sprite, I was more than ready to get out of town. I deserved a vacation, and so did Rufus. "I'm dying to meet her."

Rufus knocked on the door, which creaked open under the weight of his hand. He shot me a concerned look and called out, "Roberta! Are you here?"

No answer, but the door kept on opening. "Should we go in?"

Rufus didn't answer; instead he stepped inside the threshold. "Roberta! It's Rufus. Everything all right?"

When she didn't answer again, he walked farther inside the house. Of course I followed him. I wasn't going to stand outside in the cold.

The home was nice. There was a canvas-colored sofa and love seat. An antique secretary was butted up to one wall, and a glass curio cabinet housed a collection of Precious Moments figurines.

Huh. I didn't know that witches liked Precious Moments. Would wonders never cease?

I swiveled to the right and gasped. I grabbed Rufus's arm. "Is that Roberta?"

His gaze darted to where I pointed. Lying on the floor, dead eyes staring to the ceiling, brown hair swirling around her face, lay a woman.

"That's her." Rufus knelt beside her body. "There's a note."

A white sheet of paper had been placed on top of a very dead Roberta. Printed in black letters were the words, I'M COMING FOR ALL OF YOU.

I sucked air. Oh no. Someone or something was coming for all of us —every witch and wizard in our town.

Would we ever be safe again?

~

Clementine's adventures continue in HOME TOWN MAGIC.

Be sure to sign up for my newsletter so that you never miss a release. Click HERE to sign up!

Plus, join my private Facebook group, the Bless Your Witch Club. There you will receive sneak peaks at books, be the first to receive special giveaway offers and watch as I interview other authors that you love. But it's only available in the club, so join HERE.

And…I love to hear from you! Please feel free to drop me a line anytime. You can email me amy@amyboylesauthor.com.

ALSO BY AMY BOYLES

SERIES READING ORDER

A MAGICAL RENOVATION MYSERY

WITCHER UPPER

RENOVATION SPELL

DEMOLITION PREMONITION

WITCHER UPPER CHRISTMAS

BARN BEWITCHMENT

SHIPLAP AND SPELL HUNTING

MUDROOM MYSTIC

WITCH IT OR LIST IT

PANTRY PRANKSTER

HOME TOWN MAGIC

LOST SOUTHERN MAGIC

(Takes place following the events of Southern Magic Wedding. This is a Sweet Tea Witches, Southern Belles and Spells, Southern Ghost Wrangles and Bless Your Witch Crossover)

THE GOLD TOUCH THAT WENT CATTYWAMPUS

THE YELLOW-BELLIED SCAREDY CAT

A MESS OF SIRENS

KNEE-HIGH TO A THIEF

BELLES AND SPELLS MATCHMAKER MYSTERY

DEADLY SPELLS AND A SOUTHERN BELLE

CURSED BRIDES AND ALIBIS

MAGICAL DAMES AND DATING GAMES

SOME PIG AND A MUMMY DIG

SWEET TEA WITCH MYSTERIES

SOUTHERN MAGIC

SOUTHERN SPELLS

SOUTHERN MYTHS

SOUTHERN SORCERY

SOUTHERN CURSES

SOUTHERN KARMA

SOUTHERN MAGIC THANKSGIVING

SOUTHERN MAGIC CHRISTMAS

SOUTHERN POTIONS

SOUTHERN FORTUNES

SOUTHERN HAUNTINGS

SOUTHERN WANDS

SOUTHERN CONJURING

SOUTHERN WISHES

SOUTHERN DREAMS

SOUTHERN MAGIC WEDDING

SOUTHERN OMENS

SOUTHERN JINXED

SOUTHERN BEGINNINGS

SOUTHERN MYSTICS

SOUTHERN CAULDRONS

SOUTHERN HOLIDAY

SOUTHERN ENCHANTED

SOUTHERN GHOST WRANGLER MYSTERIES

SOUL FOOD SPIRITS

HONEYSUCKLE HAUNTING

THE GHOST WHO ATE GRITS (Crossover with Pepper and Axel from Sweet
Tea Witches)

BACKWOODS BANSHEE

MISTLETOE AND SPIRITS

BLESS YOUR WITCH SERIES

SCARED WITCHLESS

KISS MY WITCH

QUEEN WITCH

QUIT YOUR WITCHIN'

FOR WITCH'S SAKE

DON'T GIVE A WITCH

WITCH MY GRITS

FRIED GREEN WITCH

SOUTHERN WITCHING

Y'ALL WITCHES

HOLD YOUR WITCHES

SOUTHERN SINGLE MOM PARANORMAL MYSTERIES

The Witch's Handbook to Hunting Vampires

The Witch's Handbook to Catching Werewolves

The Witch's Handbook to Trapping Demons

ABOUT THE AUTHOR

Hey, I'm Amy,

I write books for folks who crave laugh-out-loud paranormal mysteries. I help bring humor into readers' lives. I've got a Pharm D in pharmacy, a BA in Creative Writing and a Masters in Life.

And when I'm not writing or chasing around two small children (one of which is four going on thirteen), I can be found antique shopping for a great deal, getting my roots touched up (because that's an every four week job) and figuring out when I can get back to Disney World.

If you're dying to know more about my wacky life, here are three things you don't know about me.

—In college I spent a semester at Marvel Comics working in the X-Men office.

—I worked at Carnegie Hall.

—I grew up in a barbecue restaurant—literally. My parents owned one.

If you want to reach out to me—and I love to hear from readers—you can email me at amyboylesauthor@gmail.com.

Happy reading!